The Adventures
of
Ali BinAar

ISBN Print: 978-1-9175290-8-2
ISBN eBook: 978-1-7384322-7-1
Year: 2024

GULF BOOK
SERVICES
Published by
Gulf Book Service Ltd
20-22 Wenlock Road, London
NI 7GU
UK
Email: info@gulfbooks.co.uk

Designed by: New Tech FZE

ABOUT THE AUTHOR

Consultant, Trainer, Mentor and Author

Saad E. Abbas

MBA, PMP, AMI-USCI, RACMC, CLC, CCMC, CIC, FGLC, SGC, ECMC, CCEPRM, AFIIBI, RMIFIC, DEIB (Finance), ICDL, MAD, QMS-LA, MBAD, DQA-TL, ADAGEP-TL, IAA-A, DHDA (Assessor Trainer), BIT & BLSI (ASHI), BLST & ALST (AHA), NAEMSE, MFAI & MI (PADI), IT (ISEA), HSAI (HSA)

Degrees and Certifications:

- (MBA) Financial Wealth Management, University of Hull UK.
- (PMP) Project Management Professional
- (AMI-USCI) American Management Institute US Certified Instructor
- (RACMC) Risk and Crisis Management Consultant
- (CLC) Certified Life Coach
- (CCMC) Certified Career Management Coach
- (CIC) Certified Innovation Consultant
- (FGLC) Future Government Leader Constultant
- (SGC) Smart Government Consultant
- (ECMC) Event and Conference Management Consultant
- (CCEPRM) Certified Consultant in Electronic PR & Media
- (AFIIBI) Associate Fellow Institute of Islamic Banking & Insurance
- (RMIFC) Risk Management Islamic Financial Institutions Consultant
- (DQA) Dubai Quality Award, (SKEA) Sheikh Khalifa Excellence Award (ADAEGPTL) Abu Dhabi Award for Excellence in Government Performance Team Leader.

Work Experience:

- 20 Years Experience in Banks (National Bank of Dubai - ABN AMRO Bank – Barclays Bank – Emirates Bank International).
- Of that 11 years in Financial and Wealth management.
- 21 Years Experience as a Government Consultant and Trainer.

Training Program Conducted:

Mastering Risk and Crisis Management – Mastering Customer Service – Mastering Change Management – Mastering Conflict Management – Mastering Business Plan Writing – Mastering The Perfect Interview – Mastering Virtual Meeting Etiquette – Mastering Feasibility Study – Mastering Innovation Management – Mastering Leadership

Author:

How to Get Right Job in 2007 – The Right Resume and CV – The Right Interview – The Right Virtual Meeting Etiquette – The Right Risk and Crisis Management Plan.

The Adventures

of

Ali BinAar

By

Saad E. Abbas

Dedicated to my father Ebrahim bin Al Haj Abdul Kader bin Mohammed bin Abbas bin Abdi bin Ali BinAar and his fathers before him, for narrating the story of Ali BinAar to me, many times over the years as his father narrated the story to him

CONTENTS

Chapter 1

The Beginning

Can one person fight tyranny singlehandedly without any support from family and friends and still keep fighting without losing faith that one day he may win? This is the story of Ali BinAar, a man who fought tyranny by himself with only his wits and a belief of justice for all. He lived in the Fortress of BinAar.

The Fortress of BinAar had an army of 2,000 infantry, 300 cavalries. BinAar was a natural fortress. It had mountains from two sides; the mountains were U shaped, so that the city was fully protected by two very high walls, and the main wall was about 2 km long and the side wall was about 700 m long. BinAar had two entrances to the fortress the front entrance was a larger entrance with and 8 cannons on each side of the gate, and on the side entrance, there were a total of 4 cannons 2 cannons on each side of the gate. The total number of cannons on both walls was 20. The side wall opened up to small farms in a large field planted on the outside of the wall; the fortress had a large number of wells inside the fortress and outside the fortress. A large Warehouse was housed within the fortress, mainly filled with wheat and rice from India among other things. Making the fortress impregnable and could withstand a siege for years. The total population of BinAar was 35,000+.

This is the story of a young boy named Ali, son of Haji Mohammed, who lived in the Fortress of BinAar. Our story begins in the year 1775 AD.

Ali's father was Haji Mohammed, a lean man with a fair complexion with a white moustache and beard; he always used to wear the same-coloured clothes, white shirt and pants, with a white turban and brown waste coat; Ali's mother was Princess Maryam, the daughter of the Khan of BinAar, and she was a thin lady always in a black embroidered dress. Haji Mohammed had six children, three boys, and three girls, the oldest being Abdulla, he was the right arm of his father; he helped his father in business. The second child was Khadija, the third child was Aysha, number four was Omar, Ali was the fifth child, and the youngest child was Hind.

All the four oldest children of Haji Mohammed were married. Ali and Hind, being the youngest, were still single. Abdulla and Omar used to help their father in his business. Along with the husband of Khadija, his name was Jaber and the husband of Aysha, and his name was Hassan.

Haji Mohammed was the richest man in BinAar and had the largest house. The houses in that era were very different from the houses today. The house did not have an outside wall. There was a gap of 10 feet between each house. The houses were either square shaped or rectangle shaped. The houses were made of mud and wood for support. Some large rooms had a wind tower above them for cool air circulation.

Haji Mohammed's house was rectangular shaped, approximately 100m long and 55m wide. The main entrance was in the middle of the house and anyone who enters the house as a guest would find the guest majlis on the right and to enter the house, there was another door facing the entrance, and once you enter the second door it opened up to the courtyard in the middle of the house as all the courtyards were constructed in the middle for privacy. The house had a ground and an upper floor. The upper floor was used for the family and the ground floor was used for the guests, the cooking area, servant quarters and the main family dining room. The house had its own well on the side of the courtyard. The garden was in the middle of the house and a number of edible plants planted as well as flowers next to the entrance of the house, so that all the guests will be greeted with the sweet smell of flowers and beautiful colours.

As this was a large family, every family had a section of the upper floor for them and their children. The house was constructed in five sections. As the sons normally would stay with their parents and the daughters stay with their husbands in their husband's family homes, Ali stayed in the section of the house that was meant for him and his family when he got married. Hind, the youngest daughter, who was still unmarried stayed in the room next to her parents' room.

As a child, Ali was a very inquisitive child. He used to ask questions that his parents had a very difficult time answering. He had a big imagination; he always used to imagine that he was a hero helping people whenever they needed help. His imagination helped him connect the dots long before his older siblings were able to understand the situation. He was an explorer who loved to learn about new things. He had one problem, as he was hyperactive and just could not stay put in one place for a long time. As his interests were so different from all his friends, he used to end up playing by himself. He had friends but none of them were close friends that he could share his feelings with.

Ali was his mother's favourite; she would always protect him from his father's anger. Haji Mohammed always felt that his son Ali was a good for nothing spoiled brat. Ali was 18 years old, a dreamer living in his own world, the job he was learning was how to become a merchant from his father and elder brothers, this was the job he used to hate doing the most. In his free time, Ali used to go outside the fortress with his horse and practise his fighting skills. Ali had a black Arabian horse; his father got the horse for him from the city of Basra in Iraq. It was completely black with a white star on its forehead. Ali's horse was one of the fastest horses in the Province. When it walked it looked like it was dancing, it had a habit of sometimes walking sideways. Ali called his horse Thunder as it was Black in colour and all you could hear in the dark was the thunder of its hooves coming towards you in a very frightening way.

Ali was great with a sword as he used an Indian sword called Muhannad. The Muhannad is a curved lightweight sword and is very sharp. Ali was also an excellent rider and marksman with a musket and a pistol. He used to practise how to become a warrior. On a daily basis, he also used to create battle plans and how to fight battles with the least number of losses. His main objective to fighting was not to lose any men during any battle that he may be a part of.

Haji Mohammed was a very famous merchant; he sold rice and grains that he imported from India; the goods arrived in the port city of Linga and then by caravan they were brought to the fortress of BinAar. He was the wealthiest merchant in BinAar. His wife Maryam was the daughter of Khan Essa, who ruled the Fortress of BinAar. Khan Essa was a good man he took utmost care of the people looking after their every need, and all the people in BinAar were happy during his reign. As Khan Essa got older, his son Khan Marwan started helping his old father by ruling in his father's place.

In the year 1770, Khan Essa died after being sick for almost two years, during that time Ali was 13 years old. Ali's uncle Khan Marwan, the son of Khan Essa, became the new Khan of BinAar. Khan Marwan was not like his father. The new Khan did not think of the people's happiness, nor did he care about what happened to them. All he cared about was his pleasure and the accumulation of wealth.

Slowly the new Khan's grip got stronger, and he started to squeeze the people by raising their taxes. During the reign of his father Khan Essa, the tax was 1 gold dinar per person per year. At first, it remained the same but within a year the tax went up to 2 gold dinars per person per year. This was doubled again in the next year to 4 gold dinars per person per year. By 1775, the tax had risen to 10 gold dinars per person per year.

Many people were unable to pay that amount, so they used to ask Haji Mohammed for his help as he was well known to be a kind and helpful man. A family of five, a husband, wife and three children had to pay 50 gold dinars and that was a lot of money for a family whose only source of income was daily labour and that would be approximately 3 to 4 Gold dinars per month.

THE BIG CHANGE

Ali was not one for thinking about politics. But, one day, it all changed for Ali; as he was leaving his house one day, he saw the soldiers dragging his old neighbour Haji Mahmoud, out of his house and whipping him on the street. He was surprised at this as this was the first time, he had come face to face with his uncle's brutality. He asked the guards to stop whipping Haji Mahmoud. They stopped and said that this was not his concern. Ali said, 'What crime is Haji Mahmoud accused of doing to deserve such punishment?' The soldiers said, 'He didn't pay his taxes'. So, Ali asked them, 'How much did Haji Mahmoud have to pay in taxes', and the solders responded, 'A house of 6 people with 10 gold dinars per person was 60 gold dinars'. Ali promptly took out his money bag and gave them 60 gold dinars.

As the soldiers were leaving, he heard one of them say, 'He is lucky that he is the nephew of the Khan; otherwise, I would have whipped him for interfering in our work, what insolence'. Ali could not believe what was happening. As he helped Haji Mahmoud stand up and helped him dust of all the sand and mud from his clothes, Ali helped Haji Mahmoud go inside the house as the poor man was walking with a limp. Ali said to Haji Mahmoud, 'I hope you get better soon uncle Mahmoud, if you have any more problems please come to me'. As Ali was walking away, he kept thinking about what he saw, he couldn't wait any longer, so he ran the rest of the way to see his father and asked him all about what was going on. Haji Mohammed said, 'You shouldn't interfere in these matters my son, as these matters didn't concern you. This was a governmental issue and merchants should not interfere in such things'. Ali was not convinced by what his father said.

Ali talked with his brothers, Abdulla and Omar and they said the same thing to him. He went home and talked with his mother and sisters; they all told him that he should not worry about things that do not concern him. He went and talked with his friends, and they also said the same thing to him. Ali thought to himself, 'If this does not concern me then why do I feel that I have failed everyone by keeping quiet'. Ali said to himself, 'Islam teaches us to take care of the weak and needy, and by keeping quiet, I am not following the teachings of the Holly Profit (Peace be upon him)'.

That night Ali was full of questions and could not sleep, as he could not find anyone to help answer the questions that were burning in his heart and mind. 'Why can't I help people? Why do the poor have to pay taxes? Why can't the people be given more time to pay if they don't have the money? Why do they have to have the taxes at 10 gold dinars per person? Only 5 years ago, the taxes were 1 gold dinar and now the tax is 10 dinars. What happened in the last 5 years? Is my uncle an evil man? My friends didn't say that my uncle was evil but that is what they were hinting at'. Ali had all these doubts that needed an answer, on one hand he wanted to help the people and on the other hand he had to obey his father. So, what should he do?

Suddenly it was dawn and Ali went to pray, as he was going for Fajir prayers, his mind was occupied with, 'What can I do, I can't fight my uncle that would hurt my mother, he is her brother after all? Now I understand what my father said, it is not out of fear for himself but out of fear for me and the family and not to hurt my mother's feelings. But keeping all this in mind, can I not act by myself and help the people? I don't have a wife and children to worry about. What good is all that training I have been doing if I can't save the people from a Tyrant who just happens to be my uncle'. during Fajir prayers, the idea dawned on him as to what action he should take.

What Ali did next put him on a collision course with his uncle. As an expert tactician, he proposed a plan to start helping the people without anyone knowing it was him, so his family members would not be implicated and anyone he loved would not be hurt. Ali had this great plan now how to implement it?

As Ali knew his uncle's home very well, he had an idea to ask his mother to talk to her brother for him to become one of his uncle's soldiers. So, he went to his mother first he had to convince his mother that he wanted to become a soldier, Ali said, 'Mother, I need your help, as you know I am not happy working for my father, I am not a merchant', his mother said, 'I Know my son that you are not happy, but what do you want to do?' Ali said to his mother, 'I want to become a soldier, I have spent years learning how to fight and I have always wanted to become a soldier not a merchant'. His mother said, 'What do you want me to do Ali?' Ali said, 'Could you please talk to my father and tell him that I will only be happy if I become a soldier'. Ali's mother said, 'Ok, I will talk to your father when he comes home in the afternoon for his lunch'. Ali said, 'Can't you go to the shop and talk to him now?' She said to Ali, 'When have I ever gone to your fathers shop for anything? Wait until your father gets back home'.

In the afternoon when Haji Mohammed came home to have his lunch, he found Ali waiting for him, Haji Mohammed said, 'What happened to you today I hardly saw you in the shop, did you go to the warehouse with Omar? Ali said to his father, 'Mother would like to talk to you'. Ali's mother came into the room and said to Haji Mohammed, 'Ali is not happy being a merchant, he wants to join his uncles' soldiers', Haji Mohammed said, 'What! Ali wants to become a soldier, why? We have money we are not poor, what is this nonsense that he wants to become a soldier.' Ali's mother said, 'Listen, let him do what he likes, he is young and the young always have new ideas, if he doesn't like being a soldier then he will come back and work with you, just give him a chance to do something he likes', Haji Mohammed said, 'Listen to me Ali, I agree on one condition if you don't like being a soldier then you will come and work with me and your brothers, do you agree to this my son'. Ali said 'yes I agree father.'

Ali's mother went to talk to her brother Khan Marwan about her son Ali. After she greeted her brother she said, 'Marwan I have come to ask you for a favor', Khan Marwan said, 'How can I help you Maryam, just tell me what you need.' She said, 'My son Ali doesn't like to work with his father, he came to me today and said that he would like to become one of your soldiers'. This news was the best news Khan Marwan had heard in a long time, He said to her, 'Ali would like to join my soldiers, that is great, as you know I have always liked Ali, and I used to help him when was learning how to shoot. Yes, I would love for him to join my soldiers, let Ali come to me tomorrow morning and I will take care of him'. Ali's mother was so excited that her brother said yes, she said to her brother, 'I have one request please take care of him, he is young and don't let him do anything that would heart him'. Marwan said, 'Don't worry sister, I will take care of him as though he were my own son'.

The main reason Khan Marwan agreed to take Ali into his personal guard was of Ali's age, he thought that since Ali was young, he could influence his way of thinking and make him one of his true followers, Also the Khan did not have any sons and he always liked Ali and wished he was his son (But Fate had other Plans.). Before Marwan became Khan of BinAar Ali actually liked him as he was very kind to Ali and used to practice sword fighting with Ali, and also taught Ali how to shoot a gun. Khan Marwan and Ali used to be such good friends as Ali used to confide in his uncle, and he used to share his feelings, his likes, his dislikes, and his future plans with his uncle, things he didn't share with his family members not even his mother Maryam.

The next day Ali went to visit his uncle, Khan Marwan said to him, 'Welcome Ali, you don't know how happy I am that you will be working with me, finally we will be working together. You remember when you were younger, you told me that you would like to become a warrior like Khaled Bin Al Waleed, Tariq Bin Ziyad, Saad Ibn Abi Waqas, Mohammed Ibn Al Qassim, and Osama Bin Zayed. Ali said, 'yes I remember,' Khan Marwan said, 'So now is your chance to become a great warrior.' Ali said, 'Thank you uncle, I promise you that I will do my best to help and protect the people from any person who plans to hurt them in anyway'. Khan Marwan was a bit surprised at what Ali said, but he thought that Ali thinks he is a soldier to help the people, Khan Marwan thought to himself (I will make Ali see that he is here to take care of me and my family and not the people, he will learn in time).

Ali joined the Khans soldiers, and he was so good in his fighting skills that he became the best marksman of the Khans soldiers. He was then named the best marksman in BinAar, he was also the best swordsman in BinAar, not one of the soldiers could defeat him in swordplay. All the soldiers feared him as they knew that he was the best warrior they had. This achievement gave him the rank of Second in Command of the Khan's guard. His uncle was happy that he now had a relative working for him that he could trust, or so he thought, little did he know of Ali's plans to help the people of BinAar.

What was Ali's plan to help the people of BinAar? As a member of the Khan's soldiers, the second in command of the Khan's guard, this gave him access to many places in the palace. The tax-collecting routine started at the beginning of the week. The guards were given a list of homes that needed to pay the yearly taxes. Ali's plan was to copy the list of names of the people as soon as the list was created by the Khan's tax collector. Which was the previous day and during that night he used to sneak into the treasury vault and he took the exact amount out of the Khan's treasury, this amount was then distributed amongst the power people who did not have the money to pay. The rich like his father could pay the tax amount so they did not get any help. The money was distributed between the poor on the list. With a note that said.

'Please take this money and pay the guards when they come to collect your taxes. I wish you and your family a happy life. Please do not tell anyone how you got this money as it will create problems for you and for me' (signed **A Friend**).

This was Ali's routine every week. Make a list of the names of the poor people who will be taxed that week. Take the exact amount from the treasury and distribute it amongst the people on the list. This practice went on for a few months and Ali was happy with himself as he had done something important to help the people. Ali felt so proud that he had helped people like Haji Mahmoud who needed help.

Ali felt so lonely as here he was helping people, doing the right thing, being a hero to the people, but he was unable to share the pride and happiness he felt with anyone especially his mother, as she may get angry at him for stealing his uncle's money. He soon came to discover a hero's life is a lonely life that could not be shared with anyone.

Ali was young and to him heroism was the greatest thing in the world. It felt great to be the saviour of the people, to him this was truly amazing. He grew up reading about the heroes like Khalid bin Al Waleed, who led the Muslim Conquest of the Eastern Roman Empire and who never lost a battle in his life. Amr Ibn Al-As who led the Muslim Conquest of Egypt. Tariq Ibn Ziyad who led the Muslim Conquest of Spain and helped create the Islamic dynasty in Spain for more than 800 years, Saad Ibn Abi Waqqas who led the Muslim Conquest of Persia the man who brought Islam into the Persian Empire, Mohammed Ibn Al Qassim who led the Muslim Conquest of Sind and Punjab the man who brought Islam to northern India (Pakistan and parts of northern India today), and many other great men. To Ali, they were all heroes and he wanted to be just like them.

Ali's greatest hero was the second Rashidun *Caliph Omar Ibn Al Khattab, who* is generally regarded by historians to be one of the most powerful and influential Muslim caliphs in history. He is revered as a great and just ruler and a paragon of Islamic virtues, to Ali the Caliph Omar *Ibn Al Khattab* was the ultimate hero as he single-handedly opened the city of Jerusalem without losing any soldiers on both sides. After a long siege of the city lead by Amr Ibn Al-As, the Caliph Omar was called to end the siege and take position of the city without bloodshed. To Ali, this was amazing to be able to win without losing anyone. So, he made it his life's goal to be able to fight and win battles without losing any men. He always said that soldiers had families and what would happen to a soldier's family after he is dead, what would happen to his wife and kids, who will take care of them? How will they survive? A leader's main job is not just to protect the people but also to protect the soldiers and bring them back home safely to their families. A soldier's job is not to die, but to protect and take care of their families, and they die performing their duties. It is the duty of the government to take care of their families until they can take care of themselves.

Chapter 2

THE GREAT CITY OF BASTAK

Bastak was a large city. It had a Citadel in the middle of the city and a large wall surrounding the city. With four main gates and Eight cannons on each gate. The ruler of Bastak at that time was Khan Mohammed, who was a kind and pious man who helped his people and anyone who needed his help. Bastak was an old city and it came into existence after the attack of the Mongols on Baghdad in AD 1258. Al Muatasim Billah was the last Calipha from the Abbasid Dynasty who ruled from Baghdad. He had many sons, two brothers from his third wife managed to escape the Mongol hordes and go south to create the city of Bastak. Khan Mohammed was a direct descendent of the older brother who was the first Khan of Bastak.

Since the Khans of Bastak were descendants of Abbas ibn Abdul Muttalib, the uncle of the prophet Mohammed (Peace Be Upon Him) this made their rule very legitimate and undisputable in the province. Many people who had problems in other cities went to the Khans of Bastak to get a legitimate rule, in their eyes from a true king.

The Grand City of Bastak was 40 km west of the Fortress of BinAar. It took half a day to travel the distance by horse and a full day by camel. As the area surrounding both Bastak and BinAar was a mountainous area, there were two paths between the mountains that people used from Bastak to BinAar, the longer route was used by horses, as the ground was flat, but the Camels used the shorter rout as the ground was hillier and unsuitable for horses. The longer route had a well along the way but the shorter route had no wells so the camels had no problems taking that route as they could travel for two weeks without water.

Now, it so happened that a few people from BinAar went to the Khan of Bastak and complained about the tax situation in BinAar and hoped that the Khan of Bastak could resolve the matter for them. So, the Khan of Bastak, on the advice of his minsters and the crown prince Abdulla, sent a letter inviting the Khan of BinAar to Bastak to talk about the people's grievances, and find an amicable solution to the problem that all parties were happy with.

When Khan Marwan received the letter from the Khan of Bastak, he was enraged how could his own people go to Bastak and complain about him to the Khan of Bastak, but he thought to himself that he could show that he was a good ruler and was ready to negotiate as a peaceful man. So, when Khan Marwan went to Bastak he took his best men with him, so naturally he took Ali with him and left the commander of the guards to protect the fortress of BinAar.

This was the first time that Ali actually had left BinAar. For Ali, this was a new adventure that he was looking forward to. As the head of the guards, he was always behind his uncle The Khan. When they entered the Citadel of Bastak, Ali was filled with amazement at the walls and the grand size of the rooms. As he was going to the grand Majlis (Grand Hall) of the Khan his eyes fell upon the youngest daughter of the Khan of Bastak, Princess Fatima. He could not believe how beautiful she was. It was love at first sight. Unfortunately, for him, Princess Fatima did not even notice him in the crowd.

As they got closer to the Grand Majlis, the great doors opened and the Khan of BinAar was granted an audience with the Khan of Bastak. As they entered the Grand Majlis, Ali saw that the seating in the Grand Majlis was very ordinary with many cushions that were filled with cotton all around the room with pillows as back rests something he would find in his own home a very humble-looking room nothing extravagant, and large lanterns. The Majlis had many windows to let the sunlight in. No one place was better than the rest and the Khan of Bastak was sitting on one of these cushions with other people next to him. The area was made like a U-shape facing the entrance.

It was very different from what he was used to. In the time when his maternal grandfather was the Khan of BinAar, the Grand Majlis in BinAar had a large chair in the middle facing the entrance with other smaller chairs around the room. But when his uncle became the Khan of BinAar, only the large chair remained in the

Grand Hall and all the other chairs were removed so that only the Khan would sit and everyone else had to stand.

As they entered, Ali saw that a few of the ministers and the advisors of the Khan of Bastak were present. The Khan of Bastak got up and welcomed the Khan of BinAar. Ali found a place near his uncle to sit so that he could clearly hear the conversation. They started talking about many things, after that the Khan of Bastak said, 'I am sad that we have to meet at such a sad occasion'. I have been visited by a number of your people complaining about your excessive taxation. Let us sit together and find a solution to the problem so that you and your people can live together in peace and harmony.'

The negotiations took time and they had to stay the night. The Khan of Bastak had a guest house ready for them to stay the night. After they had dinner with the Khan of Bastak, they left Ali again saw Princess Fatima and noticed that she hadn't seen him, so this time he had to come up with a plan so the Princess would notice him. He had to do something to catch her eye and fast.

He thought quickly about what to do, if he did not act now, she may never see him. So, he tripped one of the soldiers walking next to him. When he knew that the princess was now looking directly at him; he helped the soldier get up and helped him walk as the poor man hurt his leg and was limping now. That night Ali was so happy that finally he managed to get Princess Fatima's attention.

The next morning, Ali had another idea to make the princess see him. As the guards of the Khan of BinAar's uniform was white (White turban, white shirt, and white trousers but the chest armour was brown leather with brown leather boots) so that he had to do something to stand out in the crowd. Early in the morning after morning prayers he went shopping. He changed his uniform from white to black. Everything was in black turban, shirt, trousers, chest armour, and boots. His sword belt was black leather with a silver chain, on his left side he had his sword and on his right side he had his pistol. As soon as he changed, the other guards asked him why he changed his clothes. He responded by saying that he was the commander of the Khan's guard, so he had to be dressed differently from the other guards.

When his uncle saw him, he was impressed that his nephew had taken such an initiative and that it did not cost him anything. He told Ali to walk next to him and this time he was going to introduce Ali to the Khan of Bastak as now he really looked very impressive and a fierce warrior. The most important thing to Ali was that Khan Marwan was proud to say that Ali was his nephew to Khan Mohammed of Bastak, the only real king in the province as Ali saw it.

As they entered the main majlis for the second day, this time the Khan introduced Ali as his nephew and that he was the best marksman in BinAar. This information intrigued The Khan of Bastak and said that he would like to see how good Ali was against the best marksman in Bastak. So, they all stepped outside into the garden. They were told that each marksman had five shorts each time they hit the target, the target would be moved farther away until one misses. So, the first target was at a distance of 100 steps, they both hit the target then 120 steps, then 140 steps, 160 steps, and then finally 180 steps. Ali managed to hit the target all 5 times dead centre and so did the Bastaki Marksman his name was Commander Anwar who was the commander of the Bastaki Infantry. It was a draw.

But Ali didn't believe in a draw. He had to win as Princess Fatima was present and looking at him shot so to impress the princess, he had to do something bold to make her fall in love with him. He asked the Khan of Bastak if they could make the target swing at 200 steps. This was a very difficult shot and not many people could do it. But, Ali was confident of his abilities. So, they hung the target by a rope on a tree and made the target swing. As Ali was a guest, he had the first shot and he hit the target dead center. Now came Commander Anwar's turn and to Ali's surprise, Commander Anwar hit the target also dead center. The Khan of Bastak was very impressed with Ali and said that in all his life he had never seen anyone equal Commander Anwar in marksmanship.

Commander Anwar was a good man; he was the same age of Ali's older brother Abdulla. He felt that he and Commander Anwar could be good friends. So, as his uncle and the Khan of Bastak went back into the Grand Majlis to talk Ali spent time talking with Commander Anwar and getting to know him better. At night, Commander Anwar invited Ali to his house for dinner. They had become good friends, and as the negotiations dragged on Ali got a chance to make friends and to see more of the grand city of Bastak.

Ali was very impressed with the city of Bastak. He wished that his own city was as grand. But he thought to himself how BinAar could be great when his uncle was squeezing the life out of the people. His people were unable to enjoy life out of fear for their own lives and their families. Ali prayed to Allah that he could bring change to BinAar but how?

Now, when Ali entered the grand citadel princess Fatima would notice him, and on the fourth day she even smiled when she saw him enter. Ali was in love and did not know what to do. On the fourth day, the negotiations ended and the Khan of Bastak gave the Khan of BinAar 10,000 gold dinars as a gift, on one condition that the Khan of BinAar would reduce the tax from 10 gold dinars to 3 gold dinars per person per year.

Ali was very happy with this news and felt that what he wanted had happened and the people of BinAar could now live in peace and tranquillity. As this was their last night in Bastak Ali had to do something to get a chance to talk to princess

Fatima to ask her if she felt the same way about him as he felt about her. But how could he to meet the Princess without anyone knowing, this was a dilemma.

Ali made up his mind to talk to Commander Anwar, his new best friend, maybe he could help him as his intentions were honourable. If the princess liked him then he could ask his father to come with him to Bastak and ask for her hand in marriage. Ali went to Commander Anwar, told him the situation and asked if he could just ask the princess if she would agree to become his wife if he asked for her hand in marriage.

Commander Anwar told Ali that he should not get his hopes up, as many people have asked for the princess's hand in marriage, but she refused them all. But he will help Ali meet her. Commander Anwar 's wife was the princesses' hand maiden. This was a lucky break for Ali; Commander Anwar talked with his wife and asked her if she could convince the princess to meet Ali. Princess Fatima agreed to meet Ali and said that she had some questions to ask Ali, after Ali would answer the questions, she will decide if he is the person she would agree to marry or Not.

Ali was surprised at this and kept thinking what would she ask? How will I respond to her questions? Will my response be the right answer? Ali spent his time just thinking of all the different scenarios that could happen. Finally, it was evening, and the appointed time was approaching close, and he had to follow Commander Anwar to get into the privet gardens of the Khan of Bastak.

When they arrived at the garden, Princess Fatima was waiting for him with Commander Anwar's wife. Nervously Ali said good evening to the princess. The princess stared at him and said, 'Why do you want to marry me? Am I a prize that you think you will win? Did you think that because you are a good marksman, and you impressed my father, I will fall in love with you?'

Ali was shocked he never expected to be asked such questions bluntly. How to respond without making her angry. This was the moment he felt the true strength of the princess and that she was not just a pretty face but an intelligent, smart and strong individual who had a mind of her own. She was not a silly girl but a person who knew exactly what she wanted and how to get it.

Ali looked at the princes and said to himself. I will be very honest with her, and I hope she likes my honesty. He said why I want to marry you, because from the first moment I saw you when I entered your palace, I could not get you out of my mind. You did not see me then but to get your attention I tripped one of the guards so that you would see me help him and think that I was a good man. The poor guard hurt his leg and I had to help him walk all the way to the guest house.

You are not a prize to be won by me or anyone. My intentions are honourable, and I would like to make you my life partner and my wife to grow old together. And yes, when I competed against my friend Commander Anwar, I was hoping to defeat Commander Anwar to impress you so that you would like me for my achievements, little did I know then that Commander Anwar will become my good friend and he would help me meet you. I must say that if I defeated Commander Anwar then I would not be here talking to you now with his help as I would have felt very arrogant and full of myself. Sometimes defeat is good to keep a person humble.

I hope I have answered your questions as per your desire. Princess Fatima said thank you for your honesty and you will have my answer tomorrow before you leave Bastak. Ali said to the princess, 'This will be the longest night in my life as I can't wait for it to be morning'.

As the princess left, Commander Anwar looked at Ali and smiled. Commander Anwar said, 'I have never seen anyone talk to the princess like that before. Usually when men are in her presence, they start boasting about what they have done and how much money they can shower her with. But you said none of that, you told the truth about your feelings and the mistakes you made, and not once did you boast about how great you were and how rich your father was'. Commander Anwar said, 'If I had a daughter, I would love to have you as my son-in-law'.

It was a very long night for Ali, As the Khan of BinAar's entourage prepared to leave Commander Anwar came quickly to meet Ali. He took Ali to one side and said to him, 'Congratulations Ali, the Princess has given her consent for you and your father to come and ask for her hand in marriage.'

It was amazing to see the happiness on Ali's face as he felt that he had received the greatest gift anyone could ever ask for, the love and respect of an honourable woman, who was soon to be his wife. Ali started planning how he would go back to BinAar and convince his father to come with him and meet the Khan of Bastak and ask for his daughters' hand in marriage.

Ali was in deferent minds, 'Should I first talk to my mother, will she be happy for me, or will she say how can I marry a princess! My mother will never agree to help me marry a princess, or should I talk to my sisters they love me and will be happy to help me convince my father and mother, or should I talk to my older brother Abdulla? Will he be able to convince my father to come with me and meet with the Khan of Bastak? Or should I ask my uncle the Khan of BinAar, my enemy, to talk to the Khan of Bastak! Can I sink so low as to ask my enemy to help me with something so personal? Will the Khan of Bastak agree to give his daughters hand in marriage to me? What should I do? How will my family feel when they know who I want to marry'?

Ali was full doubts about what to do next, he just could not think straight. With all these doubts, how could Ali decide what to do. He felt like a little boy who had broken his mother's favourite vase and was so afraid to tell his mother what he had done for fear of the consequences. Ali was totally miserable and for the first time in his life Ali just couldn't create a proper plan of action. He was happy, sad, scared, worried, and so excited all at the same time. A feeling he had never felt before.

On the way back to Bin Aar, Ali kept thinking about what to do when he reached home, with whom to actually talk with to help him with his predicament. Ali kept thinking can falling in love make anyone feel like this. He suddenly wished that Commander Anwar was with him, so as to help him decide what to do next. Even though Commander Anwar was a person he had just met a few days ago, he felt like he could share anything with him. For the first time in his life, Ali felt like he had found a true friend he had always been searching for.

But fate had other things planned for Ali and none of those things that fate had planned had anything to do with getting married to the Khan's daughter, or was it!

Chapter 3

THE SECRETE TUNNEL

As soon as they reached BinAar, Ali was shocked to find out that his uncle had no intention of keeping his promise to the Khan of Bastak. All he wanted was money, and he got the money from the Khan 10,000 gold dinars. His uncle kept on laughing at the Khan of Bastak saying that he had never seen a bigger idiot than the Khan of Bastak. He said he was so arrogant that he thought that I would agree to his terms. 'Never, Never in 100 years'.

His uncle sent a letter to the Khan of Bastak, insulting him and calling him terrible names. Ali just stood in front of his uncle and heard all the things his uncle had to say. As he watched horrified at the situation, this destroyed Ali's dreams of marrying Princess Fatima, now how could he ask for her hand in marriage with his uncle openly declaring war on the Khan of Bastak.

Ali went home to meet his parents; his mother was so excited to see him after five days. She wanted to know all the things he had done and seen on his trip, but Ali just could not say anything. His mind was preoccupied with what was going on between BinAar and Bastak and what would the reaction be of the Khan of Bastak after his uncle went back on his given word. To Ali, a man's word is his bond, and to break that bond is unforgivable, that is exactly what his uncle had done.

As soon as the Khan of Bastak received a letter from the Khan of BinAar, he met with his war council and agreed to attack the Fortress of BinAar. The problem was that the walls of BinAar were impregnable, no army had even been able to breach the walls. What will they do in such a situation, also BinAar is self-sufficient, they have water, food and are able to withstand a long siege for years without needing any external help or food or even weapons.

The Khan of Bastak left Bastak with an army of 3,000 infantry, 500 cavalries, and 6 cannons. It took the army a full day to reach BinAar. As they moved very slowly due to the terrain and the equipment needed for the siege were very heavy, when Bastaki Army arrived at BinAar they found the fortress was ready for a long siege.

The Bastaki Army put up the camp and waited for the morning. In the morning, the Khan of Bastak asked to have a last talk with the Khan of BinAar a messenger was sent requesting for a meeting in the middle of both armies. However, the request was rejected, and the fortress started firing on the Bastaki Army. But, the Bastaki army retreated to get out of range of the Fortresses Cannons. On the first day, the Bastaki army lost only one infantry and several people were injured, due to the surprise attack.

Ali was busy looking at the situation that was deteriorating rapidly. How can he stop the war without making the Khan of Bastak his enemy? After all, he is the father of his future bride. Ali suddenly got an idea to stop the war in 1 night. So, he created a foolproof plan to defeat the Bastaki army and have them retreat back to Bastak.

He went to his uncle and told him of his plan. His uncle was happy with the plan and told him to have it done tonight. BinAar had a secret passage to get in and out of the fortress. It was out of site of the Bastaki Army.

The plan was to take 20 men into the secrete passage come out at the other side of the mountain and enter the Bastaki encampment from behind without being detected and reach the Khans tent during the night when everyone was sleeping.

The secret tunnel was actually a cave in the mountain when the fortress of BinAar was first created. The entrance to the cave was covered by a small house-like structure next to the soldiers' living quarters. It was continuously guarded by two guards' day and night everyone thought that it was just another entrance to the guard house. Not many people actually knew about the entrance, only a hand full of guards who actually guarded the entrance. The cave was naturally created with an exit at the side of the mountain that had a big bolder In front of the exit. The only way to see the exit was to actually look behind the bolder. The gap between the bolder and the mountain wall was 2 feet that allowed a person to walk in or out of the cave comfortably.

Ali knew that he had to take 20 of the best fighters whom he could trust with his life. As he had been working in the Khans guard for some time, he had already created a list in his mind of the 20 best warriors who are trustworthy and dependable. He had come to know these men very well over the past months as he had been working with them side by side. In Ali's mind, these 20 were the people whom he could trust with his secret as they love the people of BinAar as much as Ali.

Ali got his men ready, and all 20 men entered the secret passage with Ali leading them. After walking in the cave for some time they finally emerged at the other side of the mountain, they had to walk around the Bastaki encampment. It was very important to do this in total silence. They had to be very careful that the guards protecting the camp did not see or hear them or it would have all been for nothing. Slowly they sneaked to the tent of the Khan Mohammed. They took the two guards guarding the tent prisoner and Ali entered the tent alone. Khan Mohammed was sleeping Ali put his sword on the Khans chest and woke him up.

The Khan was startled to see Ali standing above him with his sword on his chest. Ali said to the Khan, 'I am sorry to do this to you, but you gave me no choice. I know that my uncle is and evil man, and he needs to be punished but you are not the one to punish him, only we are.' Ali put his sword back in its sheath and helped the Khan get up. The Khan of Bastak was amazed at this man standing in front of him with his sword drown and apologizing for entering his tent and threatening his life. Ali continued, 'Please take your army and return. I do not want to hurt you or anyone one else'.

The Agreement

Ali poured water in a clay cup for the Khan, the Khan had some water and began to speak, 'Why are you protecting your uncle, I know that you are not happy with his actions, I could see it in your eyes. So, tell me why should I go back and let your people live in misery?' Ali replied to the Khan, 'You are a great leader, and everyone loves you, I am not a leader but a warrior my main raison for working in the Khan's army was to help the people. Give me a chance to help them if I fail then you can attack BinAar again and I will not stop you'.

The Khan of Bastak said to Ali, 'You are an honest and brave man, and I have nothing but respect and admiration for you. I will give you six months to fix the situation; if you are successful, that will be great but if you fail, I will be back and I will not give you a chance to ambush me again'. Ali laughed and said, 'You are right. If in six months, I fail to deliver on my promise I will help you take the Fortress of BinAar and this time I will fight on your side and not my uncle'.

Both men agreed to this, and Ali said to the Khan, 'I have to go back to the fortress to give the good news to my uncle that there will be no war between our two cities.'

The Khan of Bastak said to Ali, 'I wish I had more people like you with me, that have your imagination and drive, there is nothing we couldn't accomplish together'. 'Coming up with a plan to enter my tent and take me prisoner in one night is truly amazing'. The Khan of Bastak continued saying, 'The people of BinAar are truly lucky to have a person like you protecting them'.

They shook hands and the Khan embraced Ali out of respect and Ali left the tent and took his men back to the entrance of the secret passage and back to the fortress.

As soon as Ali reached the fortress, he went directly to the bedroom of his uncle and told him that he talked with the Khan of Bastak, and the Khan agreed to leave with his army in the morning his uncle was angry why didn't you kill him since you took him prisoner. Ali said that he does not kill defenceless people and the Khan was an old man the age of his father how could he kill him. Ali said the main objective was to defeat the Bastaki army so they would leave. Now the Bastaki army is leaving, and no one has been killed during the war.

Ali said that I feel that we were very successful, and we have achieved what we wanted to happen without losing a single person. But his uncle was enraged and didn't like Ali's explanation. This made his uncle suspicious of Ali, but he said nothing to Ali but kept his suspicions to himself.

As per the agreement between the Khan of Bastak and Ali, the Bastaki Army broke camp in the morning and started to leave. When the Khan of Bastak left, the people of BinAar had mixed feelings about this. Some were happy that a war was avoided, others felt that their last hope of being saved was gone forever and now no one will come to help them from the tyrant Khan Marwan.

When Ali went home, he saw his father and told him what he had done with the Khan of Bastak. But didn't tell his father about the agreement with the Khan all he said that he agreed with the Khan that he should leave to save the Khan of Bastaks life.

Haji Mohammed looked at his son and said, 'I am proud of you, my son; you have saved us from a great battle. Many of our friends, neighbours and relatives would have died'. Haji Mohammed looking at his son Ali said, 'I am surprised how could you bring yourself to put your sword on Khan Mohammed's chest this is not right, you should have shown more respect for this great man. All he came to do was save us from your uncle'.

Ali thought to himself how could I tell my father that I am in love with the Khans daughter, and I wanted us to go and ask for her hand in marriage, before my uncle ruined all my plans and forced the Khan to wage war on us. His brothers and brother-in-laws, sisters, and sister-in-laws looked at him and you could see the pride in their eyes that their little brother had become a great hero who saved everyone from death and starvation if the siege had continued for a long time.

Ali's mother looked at Ali and guessed that something is wrong with Ali. She said to Ali, 'Come with me; I want to talk to you alone.' Ali went to sit with his mother in her room. She could see that he was not happy with what had happened.

He seemed to be preoccupied with something that was eating him from the inside. She asked him, 'What happened to you in Bastak my son.' 'Is there something I should know that you haven't told me yet, tell me all your troubles and let me help you get rid of them forever my son.'

Ali looked at his mother in amazement and spoke, 'Mother, you are amazing how could you tell just by looking at me that I can't think straight, I feel my mind will explode. I was so happy in Bastak and on the way home. My troubles started as soon as we got back to BinAar, and my uncle sent his terrible letter to the Khan of Bastak. I have never seen a person write a letter like this to anyone it was full of abusive words, and I haven't been able to sleep for the past few days wondering what will happen next.'

Hence, Ali told his mother everything that happened to him in Bastak and how he met Princess Fatima and the questions she asked and how he answered her questions. Ali's mother had tears in her eyes and said 'My son always remember that marriage is fate. If Allah has fated, you to get married to Princess Fatima nothing on this earth can stop it. And if she is not in your fate then no matter what you do you will never be able to marry her. But I will pray to Allah to grant you her hand in marriage'. His mother said to Ali with pride in her voice, 'My dear son, I am so proud of you, with all your troubles you still managed to save us all form death and starvation'. 'Allah has chosen you to help the people of BinAar from the wrong doings of my brother. I know what he is doing to the people is wrong, but he is my brother and I love him for all his faults.'

Ali's mother sat on a chair and Ali sat next to her on the floor and put his head in her lap, and his mother stroked his head gently as his eyes were filled with tears.

Ali's nephews and nieces suddenly came running into the room and they were so excited to see their hero uncle who had just saved everyone from the Khan of Bastak. They all just started hugging their uncle, and it looked like a big pile-on of kids.

That night, Ali had a very difficult time sleeping as he could see his dreams and his love lost forever. What can he do that will make everything get better? Can everything get better? With his uncle creating so many problems for him and the people of BinAar each day, How will he change everything in six months as per his promise to Khan Mohammed!

Chapter 4

THE SIX MONTHS

In the morning, when Ali left the house something very strange happened, everyone in BinAar was lined up on the road cheering him as he walked past, he was now the saviour of the city. In their eyes, he had just saved them from death and starvation, now everyone knows what he had dune after they saw the Bastaki army leave. In Ali's mind, he had six months to fix the problem, or they would be facing the Bastaki army again and this time they would not leave without fighting and as per his promise to the Khan of Bastak he would be fighting with the Khan of Bastak against his uncle.

The victory procession started from Ali's house all the way to the Khan's palace. Khan Marwan saw, that the people were cheering Ali for saving them and not the Khan. This was enough for the Khan to feel betrayed, and a great feeling of jealousy started creeping in the Khans heart. But what could the Khan do. The idea to go into the secrete passage and take the Khan prisoner was Ali's and the idea was also executed by Ali. But, the Khan felt jealous. That the people were cheering Ali and not him.

When Ali reached his uncle's palace, he went to his uncle to see if the Khan had any orders for him. However, his uncle had nothing to say to Ali. He only greeted him and told him to go about his duties. Ali went to the soldiers, and they started their regular morning training sessions. Ali then went to check on the guards on the Fortress walls that they were taking care of their duties as they had a very important task to protect the fortress from any surprise attacks.

As Ali was going about his regular morning duties, it suddenly dawned on him that he had become an overnight celebrity. Now he could no longer complete his secret task of giving the people money to pay their taxes. As a celebrity, he was now easily recognizable by anyone on the road. In the past, no one knew who he was so he was free to do whatever he wanted without anyone taking any notice of him, but now everyone knows his face, So, what can be done? How can he now help the people without actually being discovered? This was a dilemma that Ali had to find a solution for.

Ali now had bigger problems every time Ali went into the streets. People kept cheering him and shaking his hand. It became very difficult for Ali to walk the streets anymore. Young girls were in love with him, their mothers were now visiting Ali's mother. And presenting their daughters as suitable wives for Ali to marry. Fathers were now visiting Ali's father and presenting their daughters as suitable wives for Ali to marry. A few weeks earlier Ali was considered a good for nothing spoiled brat. And now every parent wanted him to marry their unmarried daughter!

After thinking about the problem for a few days he found the perfect solution. Now he needed to implement the perfect plan. Ali needed to create a team to help him, help the people. He had already chosen his team they were the 20 soldiers he chose to take with him into the secret tunnel. The reason why he had chosen them was that their families were recipients of the 'A Friend' letters. All the regular soldiers are paid 3 gold dinars per month. And the tax was 10 gold dinars per year per person. So even the soldiers were unable to pay the tax for their other family members.

The first thing Ali did was to have a very secret meeting with his new team. They were very surprised to learn that he was the person behind the 'A Friend' letters. They were so grateful that he had helped them and their families in a time of great need. They all vowed to work with him to help save other people in need during tax collection. This was phase one of the plan. Now they had to implement phase two of the plan to make it a success.

Phase two was to convince his uncle to keep the team together. So, Ali went to his uncle and asked to meet with him as he had an idea that will help improve the security of the fortress. Khan Marwan was very interested to learn about the idea Ali had for him today. Ali said that the secret tunnel information should not be common knowledge, so it should be kept with a very few people. These soldiers should be the ones who guard the entrance to the tunnel. So, he recommended the names of the 20 soldiers who had already been in the tunnel and helped save the Fortress from the Bastaki army.

Ali also recommended their salary be increased to 4 gold dinars per month as an incentive to work harder and protect the fortress from any spy or intruder. Khan Marwan liked the idea but did not like the extra money he had to pay. But, he agreed to the plan reluctantly. Ali was now happy his plan was falling into place. With phase two completed, Ali and his team could now work in total anonymity to help the people without being discovered by anyone. The routine started at the start of every week, a list of families was created and during the night the money was distributed among the needy families who could not pay.

The rich families in BinAar were not included in the list and that included Ali's father. As Haji Mohammed was a rich man, he could afford to pay the tax of

400 gold dinars for 20 people, his six children and their families also an additional 40 gold dinars for the four domestic workers working in his house. It is a huge amount of money to be paid but only the rich could afford to pay such large amounts of money. The less fortunate were unable to pay. So, either they suffered the whip, or they had to leave the fortress of BinAar, a place they had called home since the day they were born. A place they and their families had lived in for generations. Now they have to leave BinAar so that they can live in peace in a strange new city that they may have never seen or even heard of before.

Now after putting all these plans in place, having a team of 20 soldiers helping him protect the people from the tyranny of Khan Marwan. But all these plans, and his team working together with, his fame and the celebrity statues that Ali had achieved, Ali still felt that he was as far away from his main objective as the day he promised Khan Mohammed that he would save the people of BinAar from his uncle, and that was almost two months ago, now 4 months to go and still nothing to show for, the situation has not changed and Khan Marwan was still in command, the people of BinAar are still suffering and Ali was still busy playing his games creating a temporary fix instead of a full and final solution to the problem.

During these two months, what was going on in the city of Bastak? What did the Khan of Bastak do when he got back to Bastak and what did he tell the people about his very early departure from BinAar? Everyone was expecting a long siege of the Impregnable Fortress of BinAar, but the Khan of Basket left after just one night. What happened to the Khan of Bastak during that single night? The people of Bastak had to be informed as a great insult to them and their beloved Khan was too great to be left unavenged.

As soon as Khan Mohammed arrived in Bastak, he called his family members to a very secret and private meeting, to ask their opinion about what happened outside the walls of BinAar. As soon as his family members gathered, in the grand Majlis, the doors were closed. Khan Mohammed began the meeting by informing them what happened during the day. Then he said at night, 'I went to sleep with two of my guards outside the tent. After sleeping for a few hours, suddenly I was awakened with a voice saying wakeup Khan. When I woke up, I found the nephew of Khan Marwan, Ali was standing over me with his sword on my chest.' Princess Fatima was shocked to hear that Ali was going to kill her father.

Khan Mohammed continued by saying. Ali said to me, 'I am sorry to do this to you, but you gave me no choice. I know that my uncle is an evil man, and he needs to be punished but you are not the one to punish him, We are.' Khan Mohammed then continued saying that Ali put his sword back in its sheath and helped him get up. Khan Mohammed said, 'I was amazed at this man standing in front of me with his sword drown and apologizing for entering my tent and threatening my life'. Khan Mohammed continued. Ali then said to me, 'Please take your army and return. I do not want to hurt you or anyone one else'.

Khan Mohammed said to Ali, 'Then give me water to calm me down as I am still in a state of shock at what had just happened to me'. Then the Khan said I then asked Ali, 'Why are you protecting your uncle, I know that you are not happy with his actions, I could see it in your eyes. So, tell me why should I go back and let your people live in misery?' The Khan said to Ali and then Ali replied to me by saying 'You are a great leader, and everyone loves you, I am not a leader but a warrior my main raison for working in the Khans army was to help the people. Give me a chance to help them if I fail then you can attack BinAar again and I will not stop you.'

Khan Mohammed continued and he said to Ali. 'You are an honest and brave man, and I have nothing but respect and admiration for you. I will give you six months to fix the situation if you are successful, that will be great but if you fail, I will be back and I will not give you a chance to ambush me again'. Khan Mohammed said Ali was very amused at what I said to him, and he responded by saying, 'You are right. If in six months, I fail to deliver on my promise I will help you take the Fortress of BinAar and this time I will fight on your side and not my uncle's side'.

Khan Mohammed said I agreed with Ali's proposal, then Ali said to me, 'I have to go back to the fortress to give the good news to my uncle that there will be no war between our two cities'. Khan Mohammed continued and I said to Ali, 'I wish I had more people like you with me, that have your imagination and drive, there is nothing we couldn't accomplish together'. Khan Mohammed said, 'This young man created a plan in one night and he managed to enter my tent and take me prisoner in my own tent without losing any men. This was truly an amazing accomplishment'. Khan Mohammed continued saying, 'I said to Ali, "The people of BinAar are truly lucky to have a person like you protecting them"'.

I shook hands with Ali, and I could not help myself, I had to embrace him out of respect for such an honourable and great warrior. Then Ali left my tent and took his men back to BinAar. Khan Mohammed continued by saying. All that night I just could not sleep. I was just thinking about this young man who entered my tent made me a promise and left. As per our agreement, we left the next morning and came back to Bastak. After listening to what happened tell me, my dear family what do you think.

Everyone had an opinion about what happened. One said that he lied to you so that you would leave. Another replied why should he lie as he could have killed our father. Forcing the army to return without a leader. One said I believe him my father he sounds like an honest man. And he will do whatever it takes to fulfil his promise to you. Khan Mohammed said, 'You are right my son, I agree with you. Ali is one of those rear men that stand by their word no matter what'.

Princess Fatima was listening to everything that was being said quietly. Khan Mohammed looked at her and said to Fatima, 'What do you think as you have been very quiet, tell me your opinion'. Princess Fatima looked at her father and said, 'I agree with you my father Ali seems to be an honourable man and he will do whatever it takes to fulfil his promise to you, but do you think he will be able to complete the task in 6 months?' Khan Mohammed said, 'I don't know if he can or he will fail but I know one thing no matter what happens in six months, I will get the best warrior in the territory to join my army. I will make him the leader of my armies he is truly an amazing warrior that I can trust with my life'.

Hearing this, Princess Fatima smiled and thought to herself, 'My father loves Ali. But will he agree to give my hand in marriage to him after the war ends? Will the war end soon or will it continue for years, and my life will be put on hold until everything is over'.

Khan Mohammed informed the people of Bastak that a few men came into his tent during the night and took him prisoner. After promising that he would leave BinAar, they let him live. The news was shocking to the people, but they accepted the Khans reasons for lifting the siege and returning back to Bastak.

Khan Mohammed did not care about BinAar anymore or the insult from Khan Marwan, all he cared about was Ali and when Ali would join his army. That was his main concern. Khan Mohammed found in Ali that rare element of self-sacrifice for the common good, an idealist who not only dreams of accomplishing great tasks but also a person who does something about it. Day and night, Khan Mohammed was obsessed with one thing when will these six months be over and my future plans for Bastak will start to take shape.

Khan Mohammed had a plan for the future of Bastak. As the grand city of Bastak was the center of commerce in the province, it was getting increasingly important to unify the small cities and towns in the province. Some of these cities and towns were harbouring bandits who were attacking the caravans that were coming and going from Bastak. The merchants of Bastak had lost a lot of supplies and money because of these bandits. This was a source of great frustration for Khan Mohammed. He was continuously thinking how to remove these Bandits from the territory. Who is the person who can clean the area from all these criminals? After meeting Ali BinAar, Khan Mohammed knew that he had finally found the right person whom he had been looking for to pursue these criminals and save the Province from their continued threat and attacks on the caravans and the people of Bastak.

The problem was that some of these bandits had the support of the Khans of some of the smaller cities and towns, so they were getting the protection they needed. Anytime they attacked a caravan they ran back to the city or town they came from and the Bastaki soldiers were unable to apprehend them. However, Khan Mohammed felt that Ali was the one person who could accomplish what no one could accomplish before.

Princess Fatima was worried about her father. As he was continuously mumbling to himself, 'Six months when will they finish?' repeatedly. Princess Fatima was amazed about the fascination her father had with Ali. She did not know the reason behind this obsession that her father had for Ali. In a way, she was happy that her father loved Ali, and in another way, she was fearful that her father would lose his mind before the six months were over.

Chapter 5

THE SPY

After the departure of the Bastaki army, Khan Marwan started having doubts about the full situation. He just could not bring himself to believe what Ali had told him about the agreement with Khan Mohammed. He started thinking what I should do to find out the truth, so it finally dawned on him that he needed a spy to get to the truth of the matter, and let his mind rest from all these doubts that are continuously plaguing his mind on a daily basis. So, finally, he found the perfect solution to his problem.

Khan Marwan had a very old friend that he knew was the best person for the job. His name was Farhan the Merchant. As a merchant, Farhan had many friends and contacts all over the province. As he did business with many people in different cities and towns, Khan Marwan knew that Farhan had many friends and contacts in Bastak, Farhan was asked to meet Khan Marwan secretly at night as the Khan did not want anyone to know his plans, and that especially included Ali whom he started to have doubts about his loyalty.

Farhan came to meet Khan Marwan secretly, as the Khan explained to him the situation and his doubts. Farhan understood what Khan Marwan needed him to do. Basically, find out the truth about the conversation Ali had with Khan Mohammed during the night, and why The Khan of Bastak left BinAar the following morning! Without continuing with the siege of BinAar.

Farhan said to Khan Marwan, 'I will go to Bastak and meet my friends and contacts to find out the truth behind the situation'. Khan Marwan said, 'I need to know what was said between Ali and Khan Mohammed in detail that is very important to me'. Farhan said, 'Give me some time and I will get you the truth and lay all your doubts to rest. This is my promise to you, my Khan.' Khan Marwan said, 'Get me the information and I will make you a rich man, my old friend, you are the one I can always trust to get me the truth.'

The next day, Farhan left BinAar and went to Bastak. After reaching Bastak, he started meeting his friends and contacts in Bastak asking them about what happened between Khan Mohammed and Ali during the night outside BinAar and everyone gave him the same answer. As this what was told to the people of Bastak. But Farhan was a smart man, and he knew that there was something else that happened that night that the people were not aware of. He kept on thinking who would be the right person who may know the truth that is hidden from the people of Bastak. The information that Khan Mohammed would only share with a few people like his immediate family and ministers.

So, Farhan thought about how to meet a person from the immediate family of Khan Mohammed or a member of his Ministers. He started asking his friends who is the best person to make friends with a good person who is friendly and very trusting…. They all said to him that the best person to make friends with from Khan Mohammed's family is his oldest son, Prince Abdulla. His is a good and friendly man. He loves taking care of his guests. Farhan was a very cunning person; he was an expert in manipulating people by ticking them to do what he wanted them to do. Now he needed someone to introduce him to Prince Abdulla, but who is the right person to do the introduction. If he used the wrong person to introduce him then Prince Abdulla would not be as trusting as he needed him to be.

Farhan asked the people of Bastak, 'Who is Prince Abdulla's best friend? Who is the closest person to him?' Everyone gave one name and that was Commander Saleh, who is the leader of the Cavalry. Now, Farhan had to find something in common with Commander Salah so that they could connect, and Commander Salah could start trusting Farhan enough to introduce him to Prince Abdulla.

Farhan had a friend called Fouad, who was a merchant and Commander Saleh was his good friend, he always used to come to his shop to buy things. As he trusted Fouad who always gave him a good price, Farhan asked Fouad to introduce him to Commander Saleh as a merchant visiting from another city. Fouad told Farhan that Commander Saleh always came to his shop every Tuesday, as that was the day he did not work. As expected, on Tuesday, Commander Saleh visited Fouad's shop. As promised, Fouad introduced Farhan to Commander Saleh. They started talking about everything and the conversation continued until Dhuhr Azan. They went to the Masjid for prayers and then after prayers Farhan invited them both to lunch. Both Fouad and Commander Saleh said that you are a guest in Bastak, and we must invite you. So, they all went to Commander Saleh's house for lunch.

As Farhan was very gifted at manipulating people to do what he wanted them to do, he managed to convince Commander Saleh to introduce him to Prince Abdulla. Every Thursday night, Commander Saleh and Prince Abdulla had their regular majlis gathering. (A majlis gathering is when friends get to gather to enjoy themselves talking and playing games like chess.) So, this time a new member of the club was invited to the majlis. Farhan was so excited to meet with Prince Abdulla, he just could not wait for Thursday. Finally, it was Thursday, and he went with Commander Saleh to Prince Abdulla's majlis.

Farhan was happy to finally meet Prince Abdulla and start getting his trust. In the majlis, he met a number of Prince Abdulla's friends and relatives, they were the (crème de la crème of Bastak). Now with all Farhan's expertise and manipulations, it had taken him more than three months to reach this stage and he still didn't have what he wanted. How much more time was needed for Farhan to finally learn the truth about the most important night that changed BinAar and Bastaks' fate.

During this time, Ali and his team were busy helping the people on a weekly basis. BinAar had two soldiers who were hated and feared by all the other soldiers and the people of BinAar. They were nicknamed the Evil Twins. They were not actual twins but because they did everything together like twins, they were dubbed the Twins. Their actual names were Mansoor who was bearded and on the plump side, and Mostafa who was thin and clean shaven. These two individuals enjoyed whipping people in the middle of the street. The two very brutal Soldiers, who were whipping Ali's old neighbour Haji Mahmoud in the middle of the street when Ali passed by and saw this great tragedy that started his one-man war against his uncle.

Ali's team members were very busy guarding the entrance to the secret tunnel, and their secret work helping the poor people pay their taxes. Now after months of working together one of the team members made a mistake of making fun of the Evil Twins, that they had lost their jobs of whipping people in public. This statement created a doubt in their minds that something was going on behind their backs. So, they started investigating the statement and started following the team members to learn more about what they were up to. At first, everything seemed normal until one night on a Friday evening, the Evil Twins saw one of the team members deliver money to some people's houses with a note. It was very suspicious until the next few days when they started visiting the same houses to collect the yearly tax. They found that every house was able to pay the full tax amount.

Now they knew what they were up to, but they still did not know who the leader of the team was. So, they started following the team members until one day they finally found the leader of the team directing them, telling them what to do next. To their surprise, it was Ali, the hero of BinAar who was directing them to do what they were doing. But how did they get the money? They still did not have that information. So now they started following Ali to find the source of the money. All this was happening and Ali and his team of twenty were oblivious to what was going on around them. As the Evil Twins started following Ali, they found him entering the treasury and picking up a bag of gold and having the money delivered to his team for distribution. Since Ali was a relative of Khan Marwan, he was one of the very few people who were allowed into the treasury.

The next morning the Evil Twins asked to meet with Khan Marwan privately. As they were known to the Khan, he agreed to meet with them. They informed the Khan of everything they had seen during the past weeks. The Khan felt that his suspicions had been vindicated and Ali had been planning something. But, he needed to catch Ali and his team members red-handed. So, Khan Marwan and the Evil Twins created a plan to catch Ali and his team red-handed plotting to steal the Khans money and having it distributed amongst the poor people.

So, on Friday next, Ali was followed covertly and when he took the money to give to his team to have it distributed. They were surrounded by 100 men. Ali was surprised how did they find out about their secret mission. Ali had been helping people for more than a year and suddenly out of the blue he was discovered. But they had no choice, Ali and his team had to surrender to the soldiers. They were all taken as prisoners and were presented to Khan Marwan in the courtyard outside the Grand Majlis. Khan Marwan said to Ali, 'You have betrayed me. I was thinking of making you the next Khan of BinAar after my death and this is how you repay me?' Ali said to his uncle, 'I am sorry that I had to do what I did but you gave me no choice. I could not sit idle doing nothing and watch the people suffer in pain and agony as most of them where poor and could not pay the exorbitant Tax that you had enforced over them'. Ali said to his uncle, 'If a man's monthly salary is 3 gold dinars, and you take 10 per person per year. The man had a family of 4 people that is 40 gold dinars per year and he makes 36 gold dinars per year. How will he survive what will he and his family eat, did you ever think of that or how the people were suffering'.

Ali said, 'I couldn't see all this injustice going on around me, I had to do something about it. I had to help the people. I am sorry you feel that I betrayed you but. I couldn't betray myself and my feelings that urged me to help my people, my friends, and my family. As you can see, I only helped those who couldn't help themselves. The rich who could pay the tax I didn't help them as they didn't need my help and that includes my father and my relatives. Please let my men go free as they were only doing what they did under my orders. They are not to blame for any of what happened. The whole thing has been my idea and I alone am responsible for this situation and my actions.'

Khan Marwan said, 'Ali you are amazingly arrogant till the end. Even though you have been caught red-handed and I have all the proof I need against you. You are still defiant till the end. I can see no fear in your eyes. I must say you would have made a great Khan. But now, you will die a thief's death. I will let your men go as they were only following your orders and they will no longer by a part of my soldiers.' Khan Marwan ordered his men to take Ali to prison.

Ali walked to the prison proud and without fear as he knew that he had done nothing wrong. And whatever the consequences he was proud of what he did. Allah was his witness that he never expected anything from anyone for his actions. The soldiers who were assigned to take him to prison. Were very unhappy to be doing this job. As they felt that Ali should be rewarded for his great deeds and not put into prison to be executed like a common criminal. To them, he was a true hero, a man who helped everyone and that included their families.

The next day the Fortress of BinAar awoke to the most incredible news that they had ever heard. Their hero who saved them from the Bastaki army was now in prison. But the shock came when they heard why he was in prison. The poor people whom he had helped finally knew the name of 'A Friend' who gave them the money they needed to pay for their taxes. They were all filled with sadness as they felt that they had been forsaken and they had lost their saviour.

The next morning after fajir prayers in the Masjid Haji Mohammed got the news that his son Ali Was in prison, he didn't know how to tell Ali's mother the bad news as he knew she would be devastated. However, he had to tell her what happened. He asked all his children to be present to console her after she got the news. When Haji Mohammed entered her room. Ali's mother said that she had a dream that Ali was being lifted by the people above their shoulders and he was all dressed in white. Haji Mohammed looked at his wife Maryam and said Ali has been arrested by your brother Marwan. She asked him why and he said that it was because he was giving money to the poor to pay their taxes. Maryam asked and that is the crime? Haji Mohammed said that he was stealing money from the treasury to give to the poor. Maryam said. My son is smart, he used my brother's money to help the people whom my brother was oppressing.

Chapter 6

THE PRISON AND THE DEATH SENTENCE

Ali was in prison, he got a visit from the Evil Twins, they had to gloat that they were the ones who were able to discover his secret. Ali asked them how they found out the truth. So, they told him that one of his team members Fouad was gloating that they didn't have anyone to whip anymore. That is when they started following Fouad and everyone in his team until they discovered that Ali was the team leader. Once they found that Ali was heading the team, they informed Khan Marwan who laid a trap for him and his team. Ali said, 'I must say you are very good. You must be very proud of yourselves, remember one day you and your families will need help and I won't be there to help you and your families'. Good luck to you with what you have done.

All the people went to Haji Mohammed's house to show their support for Ali who has now become more than just a hero but a saviour of the people. Ali's mother didn't know what to do she was proud of her son and at the same time she was afraid that her brother would kill him. Ali's team, who were allowed to go by the Khans soldiers were now guarding Ali's house from the people who were trying to get in to meet his parents. It was complete chaos on the streets of BinAar surrounding Ali's home. The people just had to meet Ali's parents, so finally Ali's father came out onto the balcony of his home to speak with everyone. He said, 'Thank you everyone, for your support of us and our beloved son Ali. I am so happy and proud of the love you have for my son. Whom I thought was a good for nothing spoiled brat. Has become a symbol of hope for everyone. Please go back to your homes and pray for my son that he will be let go from prison very soon.'

As Ali was in prison, he kept thinking. He was given six months by Khan Mohammed to remove his uncle from power. Now only two weeks were left from the six months, and his uncle had put him in prison. What a twist of fate, what he had planned to do to his uncle, and what his uncle had done to him. Ali was thinking about what was happening at home and what his father was thinking of him. What is his mother was doing after she has heard that he had been arrested and about to be executed as a common criminal? My father must be so disappointed in me that I have disgraced his good name and the family's name. I am sure he will be saying Ali is the first person in our family to go to prison. Suddenly Ali screamed (Forgive me father, I am sorry to have disappointed you and the family, I only did what I thought was the right thing to do).

The guards outside Ali's prison. Upon hearing what Ali said started crying for him. None of them could talk to Ali as they were commanded by the Evil Twins not to speak to Ali or even give him any news. So, Ali did not know what was happening outside the prison. How the streets of BinAar were filled with people shouting his name. The people were all shouting the same thing, 'LET ALI GO' repeatedly. As the dungeons were below the ground and the sounds from the streets couldn't reach Ali.

Khan Mohammed had sent a spy to keep an eye on Ali. His name was Asem, who was a merchant. Asem just could not believe what was happening in BinAar how the people had risen up against Khan Marwan to save Ali. So, he immediately sent a letter by pigeon to Khan Mohammed informing him of what had happened. Within hours, Khan Mohammed knew the situation in BinAar. He immediately called his family and ministers to inform them of the situation in BinAar. Princess Fatima was very fearful for Ali; she was praying for his life and his safe return to Bastak and to her. But with all that had happened, who could save Ali from being executed as time was very short and no army could reach BinAar that fast to be able to do anything.

Khan Mohammed sent a letter by carrier pigeon to Asem informing him to take any necessary action to save Ali. Asem had a few men with him in BinAar he immediately started creating a plan to release Ali from prison, the plan was to attach the prison at night with ten men as the prison guards had a shift change at midnight and for approximately 30 minutes the number of guards on the main gate were four so this made it easy to gain access to the entrance of the prison attack the four guards and put his own men in their place then enter the lower dungeons and have Ali released, leave the prison where he would have a number of horses ready to get Ali out of BinAar and take Ali Back to Bastak as per the orders given by Khan Mohammed.

But before all these things could happen Maryam Ali's mother went to see her younger brother Khan Marwan. At first, he didn't want to meet her but reluctantly he agreed to meet her. As she entered his majlis, she wished him and said, 'Brother, you know why I have come. I am not here to plead and beg for my son's life, I am here to ask you for one favour as your older sister. This is not just my request but the request of the people of BinAar. Don't kill Ali, he is young, and the young make mistakes. It is our duty as elders to be forgiving. Be a great leader and just banish him from BinAar. This will make me sad to be far away from my little baby, but at least I will know that my son is alive and well living in another city'.

Khan Marwan thought about what his sister said, and it made great sense to him. So, he agreed to banish Ali from BinAar in the morning. As he also did not wish to kill his nephew, no matter what Ali Had done Khan Marwan always loved Ali as his own son. But with Ali's actions it was very difficult not to punish him. As Ali's mother left her brothers majlis she informed everyone that Ali would not be executed but he would be banished from BinAar forever. Upon hearing this, the people of BinAar started going home thanking Allah for his great mercy and saving Ali. They all hoped that Ali would return one day and save them again but this time forever. Without knowing or planning it, Ali had become the hope of the people. The person they knew and trusted beyond a doubt who would never forsake them no matter what happened in the present or in the future.

Asem heard the good news that Ali would be set free in the morning and banished. So, the plan to get Ali released at midnight was cancelled. To see what was going to happen in the morning. Ali still didn't know what was happening and that he was going to be set free in the morning. It was a very rough night for Ali, as he could not sleep. As a matter of fact, it was a rough night for the people of BinAar as most of the people could not sleep that night thinking of the man who helped them in a time of need without asking for anything or any recognition, the people's saviour was going to be banished from BinAar forever. This was something that the people could not agree to.

THE EXILE FROM BINAAR

In the morning, Khan Marwan asked the guards to bring Ali to the main courtyard, as he wished to tell him the good news himself. As Ali was brought before him in chains, he said to Ali, 'Your mother my sister Maryam came to see me last night to beg for your life. So, I granted her a wish not to kill you but, to banish you from BinAar, I hope you are happy with what you have done. You have made your mother miserable, and you have created a rift between me and my sister'. Ali said to his uncle, 'I thank you for my life. I am sorry it came to this, but I had no choice. I had to follow my conscience, I did what I thought was right and I didn't think of the consequences to my family'.

Khan Marwan asked his soldiers to take him to the main gate and release him never to come back. The soldiers walked Ali to the main gate and everyone in BinAar came out to see him leave their city. It was a sad day for everyone as they were losing their hero and saviour. As they walked behind him, they were shouting. Go and come back as you are the one who will save us, we will pray for your quick return. Ali, we love you, please don't forsake us. As they reached the main gate Ali found his family waiting for him at the gate. Ali hugged his mother and said, 'Thank you mother for saving me. I am sorry to leave you, but I will try to see you very soon'. Haji Mohammed for the first time showed Ali that he was so proud of him. He embraced him and said, 'son I am proud of you. Because of you I can now raise my head when I walk through the streets of BinAar. You have shown me that to fight for the weak and the hopeless gives you faith in yourself and strength to continue fighting.

Haji Mohammed said to Ali, 'My dear son, I see my father in you he was just like you very impulsive and ready to fight. He was also a very bad merchant he hated the job of buying and selling goods just like you. I was the one who made our business grow, I used to tell my father why don't you like being a merchant, and he used to say, I love helping people more, and when they come asking me for help how could I say no to them'. Ali was shocked to finally understand who he actually is, and that he is just like his own grandfather. Ali said, 'Why didn't you tell me this before, I always thought why am I so very different from you and my brothers'.

Ali embraced his family one by one. His brother Omar had brought his horse for him with food and money to help him start a new life in another city. As Ali climbed onto his horse, he looked at his father and said, 'Father, I am sorry for all the pain I have caused you in the past. But I have a greater destiny to fulfil. I will no longer be known to the people as Ali Bin Mohammed, but I will be known from now and evermore as Ali BinAar'. This will be how I would like to be remembered many years from now. As a man who had a dream to stand up to tyranny all alone and save his people without any help.

As soon as Ali exited the main gate of BinAar he found his team waiting for him outside the gates of BinAar and followed him. As they went around the mountain and disappeared from the site of the guards, Asem was waiting for him with his men to take Ali and his men to Bastak. Asem said to Ali, 'You don't know me but the Khan of Bastak sent me to protect you if you needed my help. Now, I am here to take you to Khan Mohammed. As he has been waiting for you to come to him for almost six months. If you only know how important you are to Khan Mohammed. Every week I had to send him a report about you and what you were doing'. Ali did not expect this. He never thought that Khan Mohammed had such an interest in his wellbeing. He thought that Khan Mohammed would forget all about him once he left BinAar and went back to Bastak. But now he realizes that Khan Mohammed is waiting for him impatiently. All Ali could think about was what I had done to deserve all this attention. What has Khan Mohammed planned for me, does he like me, or does he want to kill me?

Ali and his men rode as fast as they could to Bastak, they reached Bastak that in the evening, they entered Bastak in secrete as they didn't want to rise any suspensions. Ali was taken to Khan Mohammed's private majlis. As soon As Khan Mohammed saw Ali, he embraced him and said. 'You don't know how I have waited for this day. You don't know what plans I have for you. But first we need to fix a problem we have. Khan Mohammed called his son Prince Abdulla to join them. When Prince Abdulla came into the majlis Khan Mohammed said to his son, 'Meet Ali, the man I have been telling you about. Prince Abdulla said it is an honour to meet you at last'. Khan Mohammed said now we can take care of the spy Farhan. He told Prince Abdulla to meet with Farhan and give him the information he had been looking for. So, he can leave Bastak, and we can start planning our next action.

Fortunately, the next day was Thursday, and it was time for Prince Abdulla's regular majlis. They knew Farhan would be coming. As they had kept Farhan in total isolation, he had no news about what had happened in BinAar with Ali in the last few days. So, Prince Abdulla acted like he was confiding in Farhan and informed him, 'that Ali had agreed with his father to remove Khan Marwan within six months and there was just ten days left for the six months to be over.' Upon hearing this, Farhan felt that he was triumphant, and he had finally uncovered the truth about what happened that night. He thanked Prince Abdulla for all his help and support and said, that he had to leave Bastak for a short time for business. Prince Abdulla wished him well and he left. The next morning, Farhan left Bastak to go to BinAar. Now Ali was free to come out of hiding. The first thing he did was go to visit his good friend Commander Anwar.

As soon as Commander Anwar saw Ali, he was so happy that his friend was back they embraced, and Ali started telling Commander Anwar what happened to him since he left Bastak until he just got back. Commander Anwar was amazed at his friend. Commander Anwar said to Ali, 'Your story sounds like a fairy tale. I am amazed that so much has happened to you in such a short time. You went from being a hero to Public Enemy Number one in less than six months.' Ali said, 'That is exactly what happened to me. Please tell me how Princess Fatima is, does she still remember me or has she forgotten me after such a long time.' Commander Anwar said to Ali, 'What do you take her for she is not the kind of person who can forget the person whom she loves.' Ali said, 'Are you telling me that Princess Fatima is in love with me? I can't believe that she loves me. I didn't think that I made such an impression on her that would cause her to fall in love with.' Commander Anwar said, 'You did make an impression on her, and yes she does love you.'

Ali said to Commander Anwar, 'Let us go to the Khan and talk with him about my plan to attack BinAar.' Both Ali and Commander Anwar entered the private Majlis of Khan Mohammed. The Khan greeted Ali and Commander Anwar and welcomed both to his Majlis. Ali said to the Khan, 'I have been working on a plan to take the Fortress of BinAar without losing any men on both sides'. Khan Mohammed said, 'That is exactly what I had hoped for. I know that you are the right person for this job. You have my full confidence. What do you want us to do now?' Ali said, 'We need to get the army ready, we need to leave immediately before Khan Marwan finds out about or plan'.

Khan Mohammed ordered the army to assemble. He stood in front of the army on his balcony and said, 'Today is a great day for us as we will be leaving now to attack the Fortress of BinAar, and I would like to introduce you my beloved troops to your new commander. Meet Ali BinAar.' Ali said to the troops 'We will be having a great adventure together; my main concern is not to lose any member of my troops and bring you all back to Bastak victoriously. You will be joined by my special troops whom I affectionately call the (Black Devils). They have been trained by me and when we come back, I will be training you all with my special fighting tactics. Good luck to us all and may we bring peace and stability to the people of BinAar.' As they have been suffering greatly under the tyrannical rule of Khan Marwan.

As Ali was about to leave the palace of Khan Mohammed, Prince Abdulla called him to one side and said, 'Please come with me as someone would like to meet you. Ali was wondering who it was until he entered the private majlis of Prince Abdulla and found Princess Fatima waiting for him with Commander Anwar's wife'. Ali greeted Princess Fatima and Commander Anwar's wife. Princess Fatima said, 'I have been waiting to see you since you arrived, and you were about to leave without seeing me. Do you not have any fillings at all? Couldn't you take 5 minutes of your time to greet me. How inconsiderate could you get.' Ali said, 'I am sorry Princess, but I didn't know how to see you also I asked Commander Anwar about you, and he just told me of your feelings, I didn't know how to ask to see you again. Please forgive me. I am not experienced with how to talk with ladies, and you are the first Princess I have ever spoken to in my entire life'.

Prince Abdulla was looking at the situation and laughing out loud. Princess Fatima looked at her older brother and said 'Abdulla, stop it this is not funny. I have been worried for six months and he comes to Bastak and now he is about to leave without a word. This is no laughing matter so stop laughing, you are making me very angry now'. Prince Abdulla said, 'My dear sister, this man is not your husband so stop shouting at him like he is married to you'. Suddenly it dawned on her that she is acting like his wife when they are not even engaged. Ali said to the Princess, 'Don't worry about me. I will be coming back to Bastak very soon. With my father to ask for your hand in marriage. This I promise as I will not let my uncle to foil my plans again like the last time'.

On the way out, Prince Abdulla looked at Ali and said to him, 'My sister Fatima has been worried sick about you ever since my father came back from BinAar and he told us what happened between you and my father, and when she was informed that you were put in prison and about to be executed, she didn't stop praying for you. So, please forgive her as this was the only way she knew how to tell you of her feelings. I have spoken to my father about you and Fatima, and he said that he was thinking the same thing about getting you married to my sister Fatima. I don't know what you did to my father, but I sometimes feel that he likes you more than me. So naturally I am jealous of you. Don't worry I love you a lot, and I am sure we will be the best of friends'. Ali said to Prince Abdulla, 'I am sure we will be the best of friends and we will do many great things together, as I can see we have many things in common and that is a good thing between friends'.

Prince Abdulla said to Ali, 'I wish I could go with you to BinAar, but my father has other things for me to do. I hope to join you the next time you go on such a campaign like this one'. Ali said to Prince Abdulla, 'It would have been great to have you join us. Have you ever been in battle before?' Prince Abdulla said, 'Not yet but I hope to be a good warrior one day and join you in battle to free some suppressed people from tyrannical leaders, sorry to say like your uncle Khan Marwan'. Ali said, 'My dear Prince Abdulla, don't worry you will get many opportunities to join me, in fights in the very near future, as we have started to our journey to cleanse the province form all evil doing by anyone and especially the bandits who have been attacking caravans and killing innocent merchants and stealing their livelihoods'. With that, Ali left the Prince and joined his army and left Bastak.

Chapter 7

THE BASTAK BINAAR WAR

On the way to BinAar, Ali knew that speed was the most important thing. So, he divided the army into three parts. The first part was Ali and his Black Devils Ali and his elite 20 soldiers, they would try to reach BinAar by sundown. The second part was the 500 cavalries. Under the command of Commander Saleh should reach the main gates of BinAar by midnight. And the third part was the infantry of 3,000 men under the command of Commander Anwar and they should reach BinAar by daybreak. Ali and his Black Devils will enter the Fortress of BinAar through the Secret Tunnel and make their way to the main gate and have the gates open by midnight, that is when the cavalries are supposed to reach BinAar and enter the fortress to take control, to be able to hold the fortress the infantry is need, and the infantry is supposed to arrive at the Fortress at daybreak. Complete victory without any losses. That is the plan that Ali had created.

As with all plans, there is a big difference between the plan and the actual implementation. As Ali had yet to learn, the first part of the plan was stage one, Ali and the Black Devils had to reach the fortress of BinAar by sundown. They took the long route, as Farhan had taken the short route. This was done as planned. Since Ali knew the location of the Secret Tunnel entrance, it was very easy to enter the tunnel, now they had to make their way to the other side of the tunnel and exit the tunnel inside the fortress. Just before they reached the exit. They discovered a cave-in that occurred in the tunnel during the last earth quack that had happened three months ago. That is why the tunnel was blocked and since no one had entered the tunnel during the last three months the cave-in was not discovered. It was now the job of Ali and his team to clear a path in the tunnel so that they could reach the exit on time. Now it was a race against time, they had to work hard and fast to clear a path in the tunnel. They had approximately three and a half hours to complete the task of clearing a path in the tunnel and opening the main gate by midnight.

So, they started picking up the rocks, slowly they were able to clear a very narrow path that allowed them to crawl through the rocks and reach the exit. The guards outside the door were shocked to see Ali come out. Both guards were taken prisoner. Ali left two of his men guarding the entrance so that no one would be suspicious that anyone had entered the fortress. So, he had them dressed in the guards' uniforms. Ali split his men into two parts he sent 10 men to the palace to take Khan Marwan prisoner, and he took eight men with himself to open the gates. After losing so much time in the tunnel he now had approximately 30 minutes to open the gates just before the cavalry arrived at the gates.

Ali knew the best way to reach the main gate without being detected by any of the soldiers. They managed to reach the main gates, enter the gate house, and take the four guards' prisoner. It all happened very easily as soon as the guards saw Ali, they just surrendered without resisting. Ali asked them why they didn't fight, they said that they would never fight against Ali as they loved him and if he had come back to BinAar that meant he had come back to liberate them from his uncle Khan Marwan. Ali said, 'Is that how you all feel?' They said, "Yes and if you unbind our hands, we will fight with you'. So, Ali ordered his men to unbind guards so that they could join him.

It was now midnight and Commander Saleh, and his cavalry hadn't reached the main gate as yet. What could have happened? What was the delay? What could be preventing them from reaching. Ali was now very worried as within twenty minutes the replacement guards would be arriving to take positions at the gate, and they could be found out and the garrison would be alerted to their presence. The situation was getting worse by the minute. Ali had another problem half his men were now in the palace, and they were supposed to have the Khan taken prisoner. If for any reason the cavalry does not arrive, his men will be captured and in one night he will lose all his men. Suddenly Ali started blaming himself that he was so confident in his plan that he neglected to create a backup plan if the original plan had failed for any reason.

The replacement guards arrived on time but with the help of the gate guards who joined Ali they managed to take the replacement guards prisoner. Once the replacement guards saw Ali, they said that they would also join him. So, they were also let lose. It was getting late, and Commander Saleh still had not arrived with the cavalry. Ali kept asking what could be keeping them.

At the palace, Ali's men managed to take Khan Marwan prisoner. He was furious, but he couldn't do anything about it. Ali's soldiers took everyone in the palace prisoner and tied their hands and feet and had them gagged so they couldn't alert anyone. They were all put in one room so that they could be guarded more easily. The rest of the soldiers were distributed thought the palace to monitor if anyone should enter the palace unexpectedly. Now they had to wait until Ali came to relive them. But time was passing by and still nothing, everything was quiet, and tension was rising.

The jailhouse was next to the soldier's barracks and the entrance of the secret tunnel was between both the jailhouse and the soldier's barracks. At approximately 3 a.m., the Evil Twins Mansoor and Mostafa came out of the jailhouse, and they walked past the entrance to the secret tunnel. Were two of Ali's soldiers, Ahmad and Fouad, were standing-watch. It was strange that they picked that time to go for a walk. Ahmad had an immense hatred for the Evil Twins, the first reason was that they had whipped Ahmad's father before Ali became 'A Friend'. And the second reason was that they were the ones who got Ali and his team captured by Khan Marwan's soldiers. This was something that Ahmad could not forgive them for. So, he told Fouad to come with him and they crept behind the Evil Twins and without any notice slit their throats. Then Ahmad and Fouad dragged their bodies to the nearest garbage dump and covered their bodies with garbage so as not to be seen by anyone. Ahmad said to Fouad a fitting end to two Evil individuals whom everyone in BinAar hated and prayed for their death.

Time was passing by and finally at about 4 a.m., Commander Saleh arrived with the cavalry. Ali had the main gates opened and they entered the fortress. Ali asked Commander Saleh what happened and why they were so late. Commander Saleh was a bit embarrassed and said, as it was dark, we took the wrong path between the mountains and when we discovered our error, it was already after midnight so we turned back and rode as fast as we could to get to you. Sorry for being four hours late but it was completely out of our hands, we did not know the paths between the mountains very well. Ali said, 'Don't worry, the most important thing is that you finally arrived, and the situation is completely under control'.

Ali started to divide Commander Saleh's men into three parts 50 men to hold the main gate to let Commander Anwar enter with the infantry when they arrived at daybreak, and 50 men to hold the palace until they will be relieved by the infantry when they arrive with Commander Anwar, and 400 men to hold the soldier's barracks and take all the soldier's prisoner before they awake in the morning. Everything went according to plan, and they entered the soldiers' barracks first, they took control of the weapons then they entered the soldiers' rooms and started taking them prisoner group by group. As soon as the soldiers saw Ali, they all started supporting him and most of the soldiers were surrendering to Ali and swearing allegiance to Ali, as they were happy that Ali is back to save them from his evil uncle.

At daybreak, Commander Anwar arrived with the infantry and the fortress of BinAar was now under the command of Ali. The Bastaki soldiers' uniform was deferent from the BinAar soldier's uniform. The Bastaki uniform was a white shirt and pants, black boots, a shiny steel breast plate, and a shiny steel helmet rapped with a white scarf. In the morning when the people woke up and started going out in the streets to start work, they were shocked to see the Bastaki soldiers within the walls of BinAar and holding all the important military locations in the fortress. Everyone was asking what happened during the night? Have we been taken over by Bastak?

The people all started going to the palace to find out what was going on. When they reached the palace, they found it surrounded by Bastaki soldiers. After a large number of the people had accumulated outside the palace Ali and his Black Devils with Commander Saleh and Commander Anwar came out onto the main balcony of the palace. As soon as the people saw Ali they started cheering. And saying, 'Ali the Hero of BinAar we love you'. The people of BinAar were celebrating their liberation from Khan Marwan. The news reached Ali's Father and mother, they were so excited, Haji Mohammed made his way to the palace to see his son Ali. The Bastaki soldiers didn't know that he was Ali's father, but the people told them let him in he is Ali's father, so the soldiers took Haji Mohammed to See Ali. As soon as Ali saw his father, he embraced Haji Mohammed and said, 'Father I am back to liberate the people. This was the promise I made to myself, and Allah has made it come true'.

Ali said to his men, 'Bring my uncle to me'. Khan Marwan was taken to see Ali in the Grand Majlis, when Marwan entered, he found his majlis had been changed. His chair was removed and the Majlis looked very ordinary, many cushions filled with cotton all around the room with pillows as back rests exactly like the grand majlis in Bastak. He found Ali and his men waiting for him as soon as Ali saw his uncle. He got up and went to greet him. Ali said to his uncle, 'Welcome my uncle, I hope you like what we have done to your majlis, I feel this is how it should have look, as a ruler should be able to sit with his people and talk with them, not make them stand while he sits. This is the room you should have had; you may have been a better ruler to your people, and not cause them any pain and suffering. If the people loved you, they would not be cheering me in the streets of BinAar. It's too late for you, my uncle. Don't worry, you will not be harmed. We have just sent a pigeon to Bastak that we have taken the city and we are waiting for Khan Mohammed to come to BinAar'.

Khan Marwan said, 'What will happen to me and my family'. Ali said, 'You are not a murderer, you didn't execute anyone unjustly. So, you will not be killed, this is a promise I make to you'. The rest is up to Khan Mohammed when he arrives in two days. I have made the east wing of the palace ready for you and your wife. Please stay in your rooms, the guards will take care of all your needs. Please do not give me any reason to put you in chains.

Ali had the main rooms in the palace ready for Khan Mohammed and his family to stay in. Ali had no idea how many members of Khan Mohammed's family were actually coming so he made rooms ready for all of them. Ali then left the palace with his Black Devils and went to his father's house, on the streets the people of BinAar were cheering Ali all the way to his father's house. As soon as he entered the house his mother ran and embraced him. He met all his brothers and sisters, even his nephews and nieces. They were all amazed at what he had done so fast. Nobody expected him to do what he did in such a short time. His whole family thought that they may never see him again. But he is back in less than a week and he is now in control of BinAar.

Ali said, 'I wanted to talk to my father alone,' so he and his father went to the next room and Ali said to his father. 'I need to tell you something, it is very important to me. I have informed my mother, but I didn't know how to tell you all about it'. Haji Mohammed smiled and spoke. 'Yes, I know all about it, you want to marry Princess Fatima the daughter of Khan Mohammed'. Ali said to his father, 'Mother told you'. But when Haji Mohammed said, 'You remember the day you came home after you defeated Khan Mohammed and made him go back. You talked with your mother and all the children saw you in tears. They told me that you were crying. So that night I asked your mother to tell me the truth, and she did tell me. I then asked her not to tell you that I know. I waited for you to tell me for so many months but you didn't so I said to myself you will tell me when it is time. I think it is the right time now'.

Ali said to his father, 'You are right as Khan Mohammed is coming to BinAar, and I wanted to introduce you to him so you could ask him to give me his daughter's hand in marriage'. Haji Mohammed said, 'Does she feel the same way about you. Does she even know you exist my son?' Ali said, 'Father, she is the one who told me to talk with her father'. Haji Mohammed said, 'In that case we have no problem I don't think Khan Mohammed would have any objections as you have just proved your worth to him and to everyone that you are a very capable warrior.'

The next day when Ali went to the palace, he was informed of the death of the Evil Twins. The only two people who were killed in the campaign. So, Ali ordered that they be taken and buried as they were killed in the line of duty, we owe that to their families. So, they were buried in the presence of their families.

All the BinAari soldiers were assembled in front of the palace. Ali talked with them and informed them that since they surrendered to him without fighting. He informed them that he would give them a choice, if they would like to join the Bastaki army and protect BinAar from any invader or they prefer not to be a part of any army and that includes the Bastaki army. The BinAari soldiers said to Ali, 'We will fight for any army you will lead; we have faith in you, and you will never let us down no matter what may happen in the future.' Ali informed the BinAari 'soldiers, 'Tomorrow, Khan Mohammed will be coming to BinAar, you have to show him fealty and swear to him your allegiance, and then you will be able to join the Bastaki army.'

What happened next was totally unexpected. By mid-morning, Farhan the spy had just arrived at the gates of BinAar. He asked to be taken to Khan Marwan, the soldiers at the gate found it funny but took him to the grand majlis, as Ali was talking with his team of advisors. Suddenly a guard comes into the majlis. The guard said Farhan the merchant would like to meet with Khan Marwan, Ali said escort him into the majlis with four guards. As soon as Farhan entered the majlis, he saw things changed and Ali was sitting in the center, where is Khan Marwan Farhan asked. Ali informed him that Khan Marwan would be joining them shortly. He informed the guards to bring Khan Marwan to the majlis.

Khan Marwan was escorted to the majlis as soon as he entered, Farhan ran to greet him, 'Where have you been my Khan.' Marwan responded, 'I have been taken prisoner by Ali.' Farhan was shocked to know that his friend had lost everything. Then Ali instructed Farhan to deliver the information he had come to deliver all the way from Bastak, Farhan seemed very hesitant, Ali said, 'Don't worry. I know what information you have come to deliver.' So, Farhan informed Khan Marwan of the full plan between Khan Mohammed and Ali. Khan Marwan said, 'Thank you my friend for getting the information. Two days ago, this information would have been very valuable to me but today it has no value whatsoever.'

Ali said, 'Farhan you spent six months in Bastak trying to get the information you just delivered to my uncle, I have a question for you, did you learn anything from the experience that would make the past six months of value to you, or do you think that you wasted six months of your live trying to spy on me and the manipulating the people of Bastak for your own gain? To get information that was none of your business in the first place.'

Ali continued saying, 'Now let me tell you what actually happened, a part of the information that you didn't know'. Khan Marwan and Farhan were now very intrigued by what Ali Had to say. He continued saying. When you met with my uncle six months ago. You were summoned by one of my team members, do you recognize him. Waleed came forward. Waleed came to you and informed you that Khan Marwan would like to meet you in his private majlis, correct! Waleed was the person who actually let you into the Khans private majlis. As you and my uncle talked, Waleed heard every word that was said, and naturally once your meeting was over, my good friend Waleed informed me of your plans'.

Both Khan Marwan and Farhan started looking at each other that they had been found out by making such a small mistake. Ali continued saying 'so then I made my own plan to spoil your plan. I sent a letter to Khan Mohammed Informing him of your plan and suggesting to him my plan for foiling your great plan and keeping you busy. We had you watched constantly in Bastak, and everyone you met with. So, when you had the plan to meet with Prince Abdulla, we let you feel that you had been successful meeting him in his private majlis, and you know the rest of the story'.

Ali smiled and said to Farhan, 'I like you are a very resourceful person. It was not an easy task you had. If we didn't know your plans, you may have been successful. In getting the information you needed much earlier. But Allah was on my side (Alhamdulillah)'. Farhan looked at Ali and wondered what his fate would be! Ali continued saying 'Farhan, I would like you to work with me, I need smart people like you on my side. I need people who can act and do what is needed without getting approvals to do the right thing. So, what do you say, will you join me in my future endeavours as this campaign is only my first, but I guarantee you that I will have many more such campaigns in the future. If you do not wish to join me do not worry, you will not be imprisoned, you are not a criminal, as you were performing your duties to your sovereign leader, and I respect that. But I would like you to join me and my team. So, what say you to my offer my dear Farhan'.

Farhan was so amazed at what had just happened and how well he had been treated by Ali, this was a complete shock to Farhan, as it is well known that when spies are captured they are executed on the spot. But in Ali's case Farhan was given a second chance, not only left alive but offered a job. Farhan said to Ali, 'This is more than what I ever expected, since you have granted me life, I will devote it to you to help you fight your enemies were ever they may be'. Ali walked to Farhan and embraced him as his new friend.

Ali said to Farhan, 'I loved the reports I used to get about you, it used to make me smile to see how hard you were working to know what was said between me and Khan Mohammed during the first night of the siege of BinAar. Your hard work really inspired me and made me respect you from the bottom of my heart'. Farhan said, 'I am happy that all this has brought us closer together as friends'. Ali said, 'believe me Farhan with friends like you by my side, there is nothing we will not be able to achieve together. BinAar is the first city to join Bastak and very soon you will see all the cities in the Hormozgan Province join Bastak. This is my promise to you and to Khan Mohammed for putting his faith in my abilities'.

Chapter 8

THE NEXT KHAN OF BINAAR

As Ali started to create a new form of government within the city of BinAar, a new tax system and a new treasury was formed in BinAar. Ali ordered that the tax will be one gold dinar per person per year. As per the time of his maternal grandfather. Any individual who is unable to pay the one gold dinar tax amount, the government of BinAar will pay the amount that will be taken from Bayet Al Mall to pay that amount. (Bayet Al Mall) An Islamic Treasury was created, and all the Zakat money will be deposited in Bayet Al Mall. From Bayet Al Mall all money will be distributed amongst the people. A completely new system of government was created. That is fairer and long lasting than any other form of government.

After working so hard to change everything within the government in a very fast manner. Ali actually fell asleep on his chair his men did not have the courage to wake him so that he could sleep in his own bed. His brother Omar came to check what happened as he didn't come home for dinner. The guards took him to the grand majlis, and he found his brother sleeping with all the papers he was working on all around him. The guards informed Omar that Ali did not have any food since he came to the palace yesterday. Omar didn't know what to do so he got a blanket and covered his brother and left the palace.

Omar went home and informed his mother of what he saw and that none of the guards could wake him, as they were afraid that he may get upset so they let him sleep in the same place. His mother was very angry that Ali was working so hard, and he is not eating his food. She said this has to stop now. The next morning Ali's mother made breakfast for Ali, and she went with Omar to see Ali and make sure that he eats his food before he does anything. When Ali's mother reached the palace, she found Ali working, she got so angry at him, 'Ali, you didn't come home last night. You didn't have your food, and now you are still working without eating anything, you will not do this again work can wait but your health is very important'.

Ali's mother forced Ali to sit down and eat his breakfast. After he had his breakfast, she ordered Ali to go to the restroom, take a bath and change his clothes, and come back to her. When he got back to his mother, she said now you look much better. I never want to see you like this again. You are my son, and you will act like my prince. Ali said I am sorry mother for making you angry, but I have to do so many things before Khan Mohammed arrives today with his family, once they arrive then I can hand everything to Khan Mohammed and come back home to rest. Ali's mother asked when you expect the Khan to arrive, Ali said around midday.

When Khan Mohammed arrived all the soldiers and people of BinAar had gathered on the streets to welcome their new Khan. Everyone was so happy to see the Khan arrive safely with his family in BinAar. The people were rejoicing in the streets that they had been saved from a great tyrant who filled their lives with sorrow and pain. Khan Mohammed's procession made its way to the Palace. At the Palace Ali, his Black devils and Commander Salah and Commander Anwar were waiting for the Khan to arrive. Khan Marwan was also present with them.

When Khan Mohammed arrived at the palace, he was first escorted the main palace balcony, were he found the BinAar army waiting for him below the balcony, they are sore allegiance to Khan Mohammed and Bastak, then Khan Mohammed was escorted to the grand majlis as soon as he entered, Khan Mohammed said, 'This majlis looks just like my majlis same seating same everything'. Ali smiled and said, 'My Dear Khan, I made some changes to this room. It looks much better now as previously it had only one chair and everyone had to stand.' Khan Mohammed said, 'This is much better as we are all equals, and no one should be above anyone else, no matter what his status'. Khan Mohammed looked at Khan Marwan and said, 'I hope you have learned a lesson from your actions. I have decided that you will come back to Bastak with me. I have prepared a house for you and your wife. You will stay there and never come back to BinAar again'.

Ali, Saleh and Anwar sat with Khan Mohammed and his ministers and informed them of what happened from the time they left Bastak, and about the improvements that have been made in the government and how Khan Marwan was treated when he was taken prisoner and what happened when Farhan came back to BinAar. The Khan was kept abreast of everything. Anwar even informed him that Ali was working so hard that he fell asleep working, and his mother came the next morning and really gave him a piece of her mind. Ali was so embarrassed that the Khan was told what happened between him and his mother. But Khan Mohammed said, 'Mothers have the complete right to say anything to their children as they always know what is best for their children, sometimes, we have to be reminded what is good for us and what is not'.

Khan Mohammed returned to his rooms as he was exhausted from traveling for a full day continuously as Khan Mohammed was not a young man. He entered the private majlis made ready for him and his family with Prince Abdulla there they met his wife Aakifah and princess Fatima who had joined him on this trip. He sat with them and informed them of what had happened, his wife was so amazed at how easily this grand fortress had fallen without the loss of lives and only two BinAari soldiers had been killed in the entire campaign. Princess Fatima said I am happy that our army reached on time; otherwise, it would have been a totally different story.

Khan Mohammed said to Princess Fatima, 'I would like you to marry Ali BinAar; do you agree should I talk with his father and make the arrangement.' Princess Fatima looked at her father and smiled. Khan Mohammed said, 'Fatima, this is the first time I have come to you with a proposal of marriage, and you didn't bite my head off'. Prince Abdulla said, 'You are right father, I remember the last time you talked to her about Khan Saleem from the city of Anveh, she was so angry I thought she was going to kill someone. But now, look at her she is smiling, I think she doesn't want to marry Ali, what do you think father? Khan Mohammed said, 'Stop teasing your sister Abdulla, I can see she likes him. I must say I like him very much. The Khans wife said, 'The way you have been talking about Ali for the past six months I felt that you loved him more than your own children'. Khan Mohammed said, 'It is not that, but this boy is like magic, I can't explain it but from the minute I saw him I felt that he was a part of my family.'

Khan Mohammed said to his family, 'What do you think I am planning to make Ali Khan of BinAar, what do you think?' Prince Abdulla said, 'I think that is a great idea!' Princess Fatima said, 'I think you should tell him first; he may have other ideas that you haven't even thought off.' Khan Mohammed said, 'I think you are right I should tell him first, tomorrow we are invited for lunch to the house of Haji Mohammed, Ali's father. I will ask him then, and I will talk to his father regarding your engagement to Ali.' That night Princess Fatima could not sleep from the excitement. After all she was about to get engaged to the man, she loves her soulmate. She thought to herself, 'Ali is the man she never thought she would ever find. Life is strange, she met Ali at a time when she wasn't even looking for a soulmate.'

On the other hand, Ali was so exhausted that as soon as he put his head on the pillow, he fell asleep. It had been a very a very exhausting few days and Ali needed the rest. Ali's mother was so excited she would finally meet her future daughter in law. Everything had to be perfect, so she had to supervise everything. She was used to having guests before but tomorrow was going to be a great day as the Khan of Bastak was coming to her hose and with him her future daughter in law. Haji Mohammed was busy getting everything ready for his guests.

At the appointed time, Khan Mohammed arrived at Haji Mohammed's house they were all greeted by Haji Mohammed and his family. The Khan and his entourage were taken to the guest majlis to be comfortable. The Khans wife and Princess Fatima with their ladies in waiting were taken to the women's majlis, Ali's mother was so happy to finally meet the Princess after she had heard so much about her. As soon as they were in the majlis, Ali's mother said to Princess Fatima, 'My son was not exaggerating when he described your beauty'. This is your home, so don't be shy.

In the men's majlis, Khan Mohammed asked Ali to sit next to him. He said to Ali, 'I am thinking of making you the next khan of BinAar what do you say should I declare this to everyone?' Ali said, 'My Khan, BinAar should never have another Khan. I recommend that you should appoint a new (Wally) Mayor of BinAar, a man who will administrate the daily government requirements under your rule. As I see it there should only be one Khan in this Province and that is you.' Everyone sitting in the majlis was amazed that Ali didn't want the power and prestige of being a Khan. Ali said, 'Our province must have only one ruler, and only one form of government, the Mayor is only an administrator and can never think of being a ruler one day, I pray that all the other cities in this province will have the same form of government under your rule my beloved Khan'.

Prince Abdulla said, 'So, you will be the new Mayor of BinAar my dear Ali'. 'No,' said Ali, 'what do you mean "No"?', asked Prince Abdulla; Ali replied, 'I am a warrior and not an administrator. I will never be a good Mayor for any city, the best administrator I know is my father Haji Mohammed, and I recommend that you make him the Mayor of BinAar'. Haji Mohammed said, 'What are you saying my son. You want me to be the Mayor of BinAar?' Ali said, 'Yes, father, you will be the best mayor to administrate this city of BinAar, I have seen how you have managed your business and managing this city is almost the same.' Khan Mohammed said, 'If this is what you are recommending my dear Ali, then I fully support your recommendation. We will sit together later and discuss our future plans.' Ali said, 'I have so many plans and recommendations for you it will be a good idea to discuss them privately before you get back to Bastak'.

Khan Mohammed smiled and said, 'That was the first thing I wanted to discuss with you, now I would like to talk about something, I know you would agree to. I would like to arrange your wedding with My daughter Fatima, now tell me do you agree to marring her?' For the first time in his life, Ali did not know what to say, he just sat there looking at the Khan and looking at his father. Suddenly Haji Mohammed said, 'It will be Ali's honour to marry Princess Fatima, he agrees even though he is at loss for words now. But maybe sometime soon he will be able to say yes'. Ali looked at his father, then he looked at the Khan and said, 'I agree with all my heart'. The Khan said, 'I was positive that you will marry Fatima, I think she also likes you'. Ali thought to himself, 'My dear Khan if you only knew the truth about me and Fatima'.

Haji Mohammed said to Prince Abdulla, 'Please go with Ali to meet your mother and give her the good news'. So, they both went to meet their mothers to tell them what had just happened. As soon as they entered the Women's majlis and greeted everyone, Prince Abdulla said, 'Mother, I have good news for you Ali and Fatima are engaged, my father just talked with Ali, and he agreed'. Princess Fatima was blushing. Ali's mother looked at her and said, 'Welcome to our family, my daughter. Ali is lucky and blessed to have you become his wife. Let us celebrate this great day'. Prince Abdulla informed his mother and everyone about what happened before in the majlis when Ali refused to become the next Khan of BinAar. Fatima said, 'I know he will not agree to become a Khan, I could see that in his eyes when I talked to him'. Suddenly everyone looked at her, then her mother said, 'You talked with him, when did this happen?' with all the excitement, suddenly Princess Fatima realized that she had just unknowingly uncovered the truth about her and Ali in front of everyone. Ali's mother said, 'That is ok. Ali informed me about what happened between you and him and that he wanted his father to come to Bastak with him to ask for your hand from your father six months ago, but things happened that stopped it from happening, you know what I mean, it appears my dear daughter that Ali was more forthcoming with me then you'. Princess Fatima gave an embarrassed look to her mother and everyone.

The celebration went on until night, and then the Khan and his family went back to the palace. The Khans wife caught Fatima and said, 'You sneaky girl, so you love him, and you have been talking to him and you have planned to get married all this and you didn't tell me, now I know that you don't love me, and you don't trust me'. Princess Fatima said, 'Mother, please don't say that, of course I love, I am sorry I didn't tell you because I was afraid that you will say how can I get married to Ali his only a soldier it the Khan of BinAar's army, but when my father came back from BinAar praising Ali, I thought we may have a chance, my father and you may say yes to us getting married'. Her mother said, 'I must say you have a good eye like your father you recognized the greatness in him before he could see it in himself, I am proud of you my daughter'.

The next morning, Ali came to the palace to meet with Khan Mohammed to discuss with him his future plans. Khan Mohammed was so happy to meet him as soon as he saw him, he said 'Ali, my son it is so good to see you, I don't know why but the day I don't see you I feel there is something wrong. So, tell me what do you want to discuss with me that we have to talk about in private'. Ali said, 'Give me the army and I will make all the cities and towns in the Hormozgan Province a part of Bastak, I know I can do it, and I will make your army grow 10 fold by the time I have finished'. Ali said, 'The first thing we need to do is remove the bad element from the Hormozgan Province as we have some bandits who are attacking and stealing our caravans, first we have to catch them, as my father and many other Merchants in the Province, and I am sure Merchants from Bastak have also lost caravans to these bandits, It is a great shame that some of the Khans are supporting them for a share of the stolen loot. This is shameful and I would like to weed out these criminal Khans from the Hormozgan Province'. Khan Mohammed said, 'Can you read minds this is exactly what I had in mind, this is exactly what I wanted you do'. Ali said, 'I am happy that we think alike and (Inshallah) Allah willing we will cleanse the Hormozgan Province from every criminal element'.

As they were talking suddenly a handmaiden of the Khan's wife entered the Majlis and requested that Ali should accompany her to the private Majlis of the Khans wife as she and Princess Fatima would like him to join them. Khan Mohammed said, 'Go with her my son; otherwise, we both will be in trouble'. Ali accompanied the handmaiden to the private majlis of the Khans wife. When he entered, he found The Khan's wife, Prince Abdulla, and Princess Fatima. The Khans wife said, 'Welcome my son, I would like to sit with you and get to know you better'. Ali said, 'I am at your command. Anything you would like to know about me I am happy to answer any questions that you may have'.

Ali was a bit nervous as to what Fatima's mother would ask. She looked at him and said, 'How old are you? Ali responded, 'I am 19 years old. I think that is what my mother told me'. She asked him, 'Do you know how old Fatima is?' Ali said, 'I am sorry I don't know her age. I never thought to ask how old she was, I think age is irrelevant if you love someone'. Fatima's mother responded, 'Excellent answer, now I know why Fatima likes you. I am beginning to like you myself; I like the way you think, I have never met a man like you before. Things that seem important to most men are unimportant to you. That is good, this means you can think for yourself without being influenced by others.'

Ali asked Fatima's mother, 'How do you know that? How do you know I am different from most men?' She replied, 'I have met many people in my life, some Khans some sons of Khans, Ministers soldiers and common men. Most of them were very common in the way they thought, but you are not like that. Let me give you an example. When I asked your age what did you reply, 19, I think. Most men would have made themselves older because if they had said 19 that meant that they were still very young so I will not take them seriously. Then I asked you, do you know how old Fatima is and what did you say. You never thought to ask. In my experience with all men is that when they get married the first question, they will ask is how old is she? But to you age is irrelevant, that means you do not think like other men or give importance to irrelevant things, I may be an old woman, but I know people'. Ali said, 'I had no idea that such a small question can show you what type of man I am, I thank you for teaching me, as I still have many things to learn'.

Fatima's mother looked at Fatima and said, 'Don't you have anything you would like to ask him? This is your last chance as we will be leaving for Bastak tomorrow.' Fatima said to Ali, 'When will I see you again?' Ali responded by saying, 'I have something to do first then I will come with my family to Bastak, I promise that I will come to Bastak on this same day next month, so you can start arranging for our wedding if that is suitable for you, or do you need more time to arrange for the wedding?' Princess Fatima said, 'My mother is the best person to respond to that question, she is the only one who can decide what date the wedding should be.' Fatima's mother said, 'Don't worry my son, I will talk to your mother, and we will agree on a suitable date for the wedding'.

As they were talking, the Khan entered the private majlis, he said, 'Aakifah, let the poor boy be, I am sure he has suffered enough.' His wife said, 'What do you mean suffered, I can never make him suffer, after all he will become my son very soon, I was just getting to know him better.' The Khan said, 'So, what do you think of him?' She responded, 'I must say he is the best choice for my daughter Fatima, I have never met anyone like him before, I love the way he thinks, he has a mind that is not influenced by common people's way of thinking, he has his own mind, now I understand why you were so interested in him, why you wanted the six months to end fast, he is truly amazing.' The Khan said, 'If you say all these things about him then he must be as you describe him, so you finally understand why I like him so much'.

The Khan asked Ali, 'What are your plans, we didn't get to finish our conversation before'. Ali said, 'Should we talk about that in front of everyone?' The Khan said, 'I keep nothing from my family'. Ali said, 'The first city I would like to attach is Anveh, Khan Saleem is a criminal and he is harbouring criminals who have attacked a large number of caravans in the Province. Let me capture the city of Anveh, let it be my gift to my bride. We will only get married after the city is captured. I hope that will happen very soon.' Fatima looked at her father and said, 'See you wanted me to get married to a criminal!' The Khan said, 'I thought by making him connected with us he would change his ways, but I was wrong, Ali's way to attack Anveh is the best way'. Then the Khan asked Ali, 'Do you think you can defeat Khan Saleem in such a short time?' Ali said, 'Have faith in me, I am devising a plan and believe me Anveh shall fall, I shall send you my plans in a few days'.

The next day, Khan Mohammed left BinAar with his family, he was joined by Khan Marwan and the army of Bastak, Haji Mohammed was now the new Wali of BinAar. Ali asked his father for 200 bags of rice and some grain. He created a caravan with 100 camels to go to Anveh and investigate the city from within as merchants. So, he left BinAar with 20 Black Devils and Farhan.

Chapter 9

THE BASTAK ANVEH WAR

The City of Anveh, a city to the north of Bastak, is about 40 km from Bastak, a strong hold for some of the Bandits in the Hormozgan Province.

The City of Anveh had an army of 1,800 infantry and 200 cavalries. The city had three entrances and 4 cannons on each gate, a total of 12 cannons. It was ruled by Khan Saleem, who was in his early forties. This city is home to three teams of Bandits, who are supported by Khan Saleem. They pay the Khan 20% of the looted amount.

Ali, Farhan, and five of his Black Devils were dressed as merchants and the remaining 15 were dressed as guards to protect the caravan from Bandits. Ali did not want to get attacked by Bandits on the way to Anveh, so he took a route not travelled by Caravans, to avoid any confrontations with Bandits along the way. Ali knew that the Bandits were no match for him and his team, but if he defeated them before he reached Anveh, it may alert the Khan and his men of his plans. It took them three days, but they reached Anveh without any incident. As they entered the city, some merchants came to meet them to buy their goods. Ali said that he would meet with them and discuss a reasonable price.

Ali and his men stayed at the guest house, and this is the name given to hotels and Inns during that time. He managed to get a good price for his rice and grain. He actually made a good profit for his father. Now, Ali had to stay and investigate the city. So, his men started to walk around the city looking for weak points in the city walls, so that they could take advantage of those weak points to enter the city. Ali on the other hand had to distract the merchants and guards so he was looking to buy things to take back with him to BinAar, as goods to be sold. So, when Ali and his team met in the evening, they started talking about the walls and they found a gap in the wall.

Anveh has only three walls and on the fourth side is a mountain, a natural barrier. But three months ago, the province had an earthquake so a part of the wall that links with the mountain was damaged so it had a gap that anyone could enter from. Khan Saleem did not want to pay for the repairs, so the gap was never closed. Farhan, having some friends in the city, managed to get more information about the people of Anveh.

Farhan said, 'The people are not happy with Khan Saleem, they feel that he is a bandit King who is taking care of Bandits. They have all heard of Ali BinAar and how he freed BinAar from the tyrant Khan Marwan, and they are all hoping that Ali BinAar comes to Anveh and frees them from Khan Saleem and his Bandits. Ali was pleased to hear the news. Farhan also managed to get the actual number of soldiers, the army was made up of 1,800 infantry and 200 cavalries, a total of 2,000 solders. Ali started creating his plan.

The next morning Ali managed to get all the goods he needed to take back with him to BinAar. Anveh was famous for creating jewellery, so he bought jewellery to take with him to BinAar to be sold. Again, he and his men took a route less travelled and reached BinAar safely. On the way to BinAar Ali sent a message to The Khan of Bastak requesting him to send an army of 2,000 infantry and 500 cavalries commanded by Commanders Saleh and Anwar. The army should reach Anveh, within 4 days. As Ali reached BinAar, he ordered 1,000 infantry and 300 cavalries to get ready to march with him to Anveh the next day. After making all the military plans with both the Commanders of the Infantry and cavalry he went to meet his father.

Wali Mohammed welcomed his son Ali, Abdulla and Omar were also present in the Wali's Grand Majlis. Abdulla had been looking at the goods that Ali got from Anveh and gave his father a full report. Wali Mohammed said to Ali, 'If I had known before that you were such a good merchant, I would have sent you to other cities to trade. Abdulla just informed me that you doubled our profits. We are both very impressed by your trading abilities.' Ali said, 'I am sorry father, but I was in Anveh not to trade but to gather intelligence.' Wali Mohammed said to Ali, 'A merchant's son is a merchant's son, buying and selling is in your blood, even if you think being a merchant is boring.' Half of the palace had been turned into a government office to manage the daily affairs of managing the city of BinAar. The other half of the Palace was kept as the Khans residence when he visits BinAar'.

Wali Mohammed, decided to give Ali the profits that he made trading in Anveh, the amount came to 10,000 Gold Dinars. Ali took the money and he gave 50 Gold dinars to each Black Devil and the remaining 9,000 Dinars he had distributed among the solders. When his father saw what Ali had done. 'He asked him why did you do that?' Ali said 'I don't need the money and my solders needed it more than me so I gave it to them'. Wali Mohammed said, 'Ali every day you surprise me more than more, I don't think I will ever be able to understand the way you think, but I am proud of you my son'.

When Ali went home that evening, Ali's mother had received the news about Ali's great business accomplishment. She welcomed him home and said, 'You see my son, you have the blood of your father within you, as you have done what both your brothers could never do. You are a merchant but not a type of merchant like your father and brothers, who sit in a shop all day long, you are the other kind of merchant who travels from place to place selling his goods, if you ever stop your campaigns, you will make a great travelling Merchant my son.' Ali said, 'Sorry mother to disappoint you, but I have no such plans of becoming a travelling merchant. I have to leave in the morning with the army, hopefully I will be back within two weeks, then we can go to Bastak for the wedding ceremony. I hope that is agreeable to you mother?' Ali's mother said, 'How can you be sure that you will be back in two weeks do you think that you would be able to defeat the Anveh army so fast?' Ali said, 'Yes mother, the Anveh army can never withstand our army, wait and see what we will do.'

In the morning, Ali left BinAar with an army of 1,000 infantry, 300 hundred cavalries and his Black Devils accompanied by Farhan his spy. Both the armies from Bastak and BinAar were supposed to meet in a place called 'Biseh' a small town 10 km away from Anveh. The BinAari army arrived first and the Bastaki army arrived a few hours later. As soon as Ali saw Commander Saleh, he said to him, 'I hope you didn't get lost again this time,' Commander Saleh said, 'Will I ever live that down, I got lost only once it was dark you know,' both armies joined together but something had to be done first. Ali sent his Black Devils as merchants looking to buy some goods to take with them. This way they will be inside the walls of Anveh, and they can open the gates during the night if needed.

The Black Devils were given a head start of a few hours, as soon as the Bastaki army was sited the gates were closed. The Bastaki army was 3,000 infantries commanded by Anwar and 800 cavalries Commanded by Saleh. This was considered a very large army during that time. The Bastaki army put up the camp at a safe distance from the cannons of Anveh.

In the morning, the Bastaki army was standing in formation in front of the city of Anveh, the infantry standing in the centre, with the cavalries standing on both sides of the infantry, which is an impressive-looking army. Ali requested to meet with Khan Saleem, but Khan Saleem refused to meet with him. So, Ali tried to talk with the people, but he was too far away and couldn't be heard. Then suddenly the Anveh cannons started firing at the Bastaki army. But luckily, they were out of range. So, Ali looked at his soldiers and smiled. Ali said, 'Be ready tonight, we will be able to enter the city at midnight.'

The Black Devils were ready and at midnight, the gates were opened. Not the main gates but the gates on the right side of the city. The palace was taken, and Khan Saleem and his family were taken prisoner. In the morning when the people of Anveh started to leave their homes to go to work, they were surprised to find the Bastaki army controlling the streets of Anveh. All the people of Anveh started going to the palace, Ali and his team with Both his Commanders were on the balcony of the palace. Ali said to the people of Anveh, 'Don't worry, everything is fine, you are all safe, all we wanted to do was remove the bandits from your city and that has been accomplished, during the night we have arrested 72 bandits in your city, 5 bandits were killed as they were fighting with our soldiers and refused to surrender. Also, we have taken Khan Saleem prisoner because he was supporting these Bandits. We would like to apologize for the death of 8 soldiers as they were killed doing their duty.

I would like to inform you that the Khan of Bastak will be arriving in Anveh within two day to meet with you his people, please go about your business as though nothing has happened in your beautiful city, we are here to liberate you from the Bandits controlling your city.'

Again, Ali started to make changes in the government system exactly like he did in BinAar. He had created Bayet Al Mall exactly like what happened in BinAar. The money that was recovered from the bandits headquarters in Anveh was distributed into three parts 50% was distributed among the Bastaki soldiers equally, 20% was sent to the Bayet Al Mall. And 30% was sent to Bastak to be distributed among the Merchants who lost their goods when the Bandits attacked their caravans.

As Ali was busy with implementing the new procedures in the government, one of the Black Devils, his friend Ahmad, came to Ali and asked Ali, 'Why did we come to Anveh and check all the week points in the wall and, we stayed for so many days looking at everything. Then after all that, we entered the walls by posing as merchants and at the appointed time we attacked the guards guarding the side gate, overpowered them and managed to open the gates on time so that the army could enter. Please, tell me what that was all about'. Ali smiled and said, 'I needed to understand the geography of the city and know all the week points in the walls, so I could find the best way to take the city. Also, if one plan failed, I could find another replacement plan'. Ahmad said, 'Now, I understand I will go and tell the rest of the team as they were afraid to ask you'. Ali said to Ahmad, 'I am happy that at least you are not afraid of me'. Ahmad said, 'I am afraid of you, but we had a draw, and I got the shortest straw'.

All the soldiers of Anveh were gathered outside the palace and Ali met them and gave them a choice, either they could join the Bastaki army, or they could resign from the army. When the soldiers were told that 50% of the money that was recovered from the Bandits was distributed among the soldiers of Bastak and BinAar equally. This showed the soldiers that Khan Mohammed of Bastak was a great man and he treated everyone working for him equally. So, after being treated with respect and given a choice to either join the combined Bastak, BinAar and Anveh army or leave the army to work privately. The entire Anveh army swore allegiance to Khan Mohammed of Bastak.

When Khan Mohammed arrived in Anveh two days later, the streets of Anveh were lined with people welcoming the Khan and cheering and celebrating their freedom in the streets. The Khans procession went from the main gate to the palace. Again, he met with Ali and his Commanders. The Khan said, 'This is amazing, my son Ali. You have accomplished in less than a month what no one has done before. You managed to defeat BinAar and now Anveh, I am wondering what you will do next'. Ali said, 'My dear Khan, I am here to serve you and to serve justice to the people in whatever city they maybe, my main objective as we have spoken before is to unify the province under the Bastaki system of government. With Allah's help I plan to unify the province from the Port city of Bandar-e Lengeh to the Grand City of Bastak as You are the legitimate ruler of the province, this province must have only one Khan and that is you and your descendants. The rest of the cities must have a (Waly) Mayor'.

Now, they had to find a new (Waly) Mayor for Anveh. Ali asked Farhan you are the best person to find us a new Wali a good and honest man who knows how to administrate the governmental duties of Anveh. As Farhan knew the people of Anveh, he had also heard of a merchant called Ebrahim, who was an honest man and was a good administrator. So, Ebrahim, the Merchant, was invited to the palace, he was met by Khan Mohammed and Ali, they talked to him and offered him the position of Wali of Anveh. Reluctantly Ebrahim agreed. Ali informed him, 'That he needed to start his Mayoral duties from the next day.'

Then Khan Mohammed met Khan Saleem. As soon as Khan Saleem entered the majlis and he saw Khan Mohammed and Ali, he looked at Ali and said, 'You are Ali, the hero of BinAar.' Ali responded by saying, 'I am Ali.' 'How did you manage to enter my city so fast? I never thought that you could do it, especially that you did not have any cannons with you.' Ali said, 'In war, you have to out think your enemy and that is what we did we knew that we didn't need any cannons to fight this war. All we needed was to get the gates open, and that is exactly what we had done. Once the gates were opened the army managed to enter the city without being detected. Taking the palace was very easy. You only had 4 guards around the palace. My Black Devils took them prisoner before the main army entered the city.' Ali continued saying, 'I would have expected you to be awake and creating plans to protect the city from us, but you had gone to bed without a worry in the world, your bad planning and underestimating the Bastaki army put you in this predicament. The best part was that my soldiers took you prisoner as you slept. Did you think that by ignoring our army and firing your cannons you will get rid of us so easily? Your actions proved to us that you are a bad Khan and you do not deserve to be a Khan or rule anyone.'

Khan Mohammed looked at Khan Saleem and said, 'I can't believe that I had considered giving my daughter Fatima's hand in marriage to you. I am very happy that she rejected you then.' Then Khan Mohammed continued saying, 'I have decided that you and your family will come and stay in Bastak next to Marwan, the ex-Khan of BinAar. You will have my protection, but you will never be allowed to come back to Anveh. Regarding the Bandits they will be tried and punished as per the severity of their individual actions'.

Khan Mohammed sat with Ali; he asked him, 'What are your plans Ali.' Ali responded, 'I am planning to make a clear path from Bastak to (Bandar-e Lengeh), the Port city of Lengeh. So, all goods that pass through this area from Bandar-e Lengeh to Bastak and the surrounding cities should be safe from any Bandit attack. I am sure that once the Bandits see what was happening around them, they would start to leave the province, instead of thinking of fighting our armies, they would just get up and leave this place forever. And if they don't leave of their own accord, they will have to face the consequences'. Khan Mohammed said, 'You have big plans can you do what you are planning to do in such a short time?' Ali looked at him and said, 'I plan to have all these cities under the control of Bastak in less than one year. You have the army I need, and I have the ability to make our dream come true my Khan.'

Khan Mohammed said, 'I am happy with all your plans, but when will you start implementing your plans my son.' Ali said, 'I plan to start attacking the cities one by one after the wedding of course with your permission my Khan.' Khan Mohammed said, 'The army will be under your command whenever you need them.' Ali said, 'I plan to mix the army from each city we conquer I believe that a mixed army will function better as they will all feel a part of the hole and not a conquered people that are brushed aside. We have to create a joint community from Bastak all the way to Bandar-e Lengeh.'

The next day, Khan Mohammed left Anveh and went back to Bastak. Ali had to finish a few administrative affairs before he left Anveh. After three days, Ali left with the army. He split the army and each part went back to the city they came from. Ali reached BinAar two days earlier than planned. Ali's mother said, 'I am amazed at how you managed to conquer cities without losing any men, I have never heard of wars being fought the way you fight your wars'. But Ali was so exhausted from fighting and planning wars. As soon as he put his head on the bed, he was fast asleep. Ali's mother was worried about her son Ali, she did not know what to do or how to help him, she knew that he was trying to help the people, and this was the only way he knew how.

Chapter 10

THE WEDDING

H aji Mohammed was very busy preparing the dowry for Princess Fatima, as it is the custom in the Islamic world that the man has to give an agreed dowry to his wife. Since it was Ali who was getting married Haji Mohammed, had to help his son pay the dowry amount as that is one of the duties of the groom. Ali's mother on the other side was preparing the gifts of clothes and jewellery that Ali would present to Princess Fatima. No husband can meet his bride empty-handed so the gift of clothes and jewellery must be prepared in advance.

As the preparations for the wedding were going on suddenly Farhan came running to Ali. Farhan said, 'I just got the news that the bandits in the city of Herang that is under the protection of Khan Mirza from the city of Kookherd are planning to attack the wedding caravan once it leaves BinAar in two weeks'. Farhan continued saying, 'Khan Mirza who is an evil man had given his blessing to the bandits that he fully supports this unprovoked attack on you and your family, he has informed the bandits that everyone in the wedding caravan should be killed'.

Ali was shocked to learn of this dastardly plan of Khan Mirza. Ali asked Farhan, 'Are you sure of this information?' Farhan responded, 'Yes, I have my trusted people in every city in this province, so if any Khan has any planes to attack us or do anything to harm us, I will be informed'. Ali said, 'We have ten days to attack Herang and Kookherd'. Ali said to Farhan, 'Get me a detailed plan of both cities Herang and Kookherd and I will also need to know the size of the armies and all military information such as guns and cannons this will help me create a battle plan and the best way to attack both cities at the same time and capture Khan Mirza.' Ali continued saying, 'This man plans to kill me and my family, but I will be merciful and just kill him and not his family, this I swear that I will make sure that no harm comes to his family'.

Ali sent riders with letters to Bastak and Anveh requesting all the solders from both cities should be sent to BinAar without any delay. As soon as the riders

reached Bastak and Anveh both armies were sent to BinAar on the spot. It took both armies to reach BinAar a total of 2 days. The BinAari army was also made ready to leave as soon as the other 2 armies arrived. All 3 armies joined together and departed BinAar.

Farhan informed Ali of the layout of both cities, and that Herang had an army strength of 500 infantry, 6 cannons, and more than 100 bandits. Kookherd had a strength of 1,200 infantry, 400 cavalries, and 8 cannons. Kookherd was only 5 km away from Herang. Both cities were under the control of Khan Mirza.

The Bastaki army had a total army size of 6,000 infantry, 1,000 cavalries, and 10 cannons. Moving cannons from one place to another was a great undertaking on its own. Each cannon had six mules pulling the cannon with three carts for each cannon pulled by four mules, these carts contained the gunpowder, cannon balls and other items needed to fire a cannon. As the cannons were heavy, moving them through a mountainous terrain was not an easy task.

The plan was to split the army into two parts. The first army of 2,000 infantry and 4 cannons under the command of Anwar would go to the city of Herang and lay siege to the city, the purpose of the siege was to stop anyone from exiting the city, especially the Bandits. The second army of 4,000 infantry, 1,000 cavalries, and 6 cannons under the command of Ali himself, would go to capture the city of Kookherd, once Khan Mirza was taken prisoner, the city of Herang would surrender.

When the Bastaki army was close to both cities, the army split into two parts as planned. Both cities were surrounded at the same time stopping either city from helping the other. The city of Kookherd had three walls with a mountain at the back of the city. It was a large city with a population of more than 9,000 people.

The same was for the city of Herang at also had three walls with its back to the mountain, the city had a population of approximately 5,000 people.

Bastak had become very famous in the province since the fall of BinAar and the fall of Anveh, and how the captured cities were treated by the conquering Bastaki army, Ali BinAar, and Khan Mohammed. Many cities in the province hoped to be a part of Bastak and wanted Khan Mohammed to rule them. Ali BinAar and his Black Devils had become famous in the Province. The Bastaki army took up its position outside the walls of Kookherd 2,000 infantry in the center with the cavalry of 500 on each side. Facing the other two side walls was 1,000 infantry on each side. When the Kookherd army saw the size of the Bastaki army, that the Bastaki army outnumber them to more than 3 to 1. This made them start thinking about what to do. Khan Mirza had just been informed that the city of Kookherd was surrounded by the Bastaki army.

What happened next was totally unexpected. What the Kookherd army did next Ali hadn't planned for. Ali's plan was to start firing the 6 cannons onto the city walls to bring down the main gate as it was the weakest point in the wall, this would create a breach needed in the wall, and then send the infantry to secure the city. Ali was hoping to minimize the losses on both sides, but his plan was to end the siege as fast as possible as Ali never believed in prolonging any war.

Once the army was in place Ali and his Black Devils started making their way forward to the front of the army. It was an amazing view from the walls of Kookherd to see these 21 soldiers dressed in Black moving through a sea of soldiers in White and Silver to the front of the Bastaki army. Once the soldiers of Kookherd saw Ali and his dancing hours they started shouting from the walls. 'Ali BinAar—Ali BinAar—Ali BinAar' repeatedly. Within minutes, the main gate was opened, and the soldiers came out running to welcome Ali into the city of Kookherd.

The Bastaki army was in shock, they did not believe what they were seeing with their eyes. Ali started to enter the city with the army and the soldiers and the people of Kookherd were lined up in the roads of Kookherd cheering and Welcoming Ali and the Bastaki army to Kookherd. The guards of Khan Mirza had taken him prisoner as soon as the gates were opened. Once Ali and the soldiers reached the palace and Ali saw Khan Mirza and asked him, 'Look at what has happened to you, your plan was to kill me and my family and you and your family are under my mercy, so what should I do with you.' Khan Mirza said, 'Yes, you are right I was planning to kill you and your family, but Allah has made me pay for my sins as my son had died two days ago in his sleep'. Khan Mirza continued saying, 'I have been informed that you are a good and just man, so I plead to your justice not to kill me and my family, as my family are completely innocent and haven't done anything to heart you or anyone, it has always been me.'

Ali said to Khan Mirza, 'It was never my plan to kill your family, but I was very angry with you for planning to kill me and my and my family so, I had planned to kill you. But I think the loss of your son has made me think that I shouldn't kill you and let Khan Mohammed decide your fate'. Ali said, 'I have one question for you, did you ever think that you are such a bad leader that your own people would betray you and tie you up like a criminal and hand you over to your enemy without a second thought?' Khan Mirza said, 'I was so blinded by my power and wealth, I had two cities that were all mine with more than 14,000 people living under my rule, I never thought that my people were suffering and that they hated me so much'.

Ali gave orders to the soldiers to take care of Khan Mirza and his family, and no harm should come to them in his absence. They were to be kept in a section of the palace they could stay comfortably until the arrival of Khan Mohammed from Bastak. Ali and the Black Devils with the 1,000 Cavalries left Kookherd and went to Herang, he also asked the head of the Kookherd army to join him and the Kookherdi cavalry. As Herang was only 5 km away from Kookherd it didn't take them long to reach. Commander Anwar was surprised to see Ali arrive so soon from Kookherd. Anwar asked Ali, 'What happened! Why did you leave the siege of Kookherd so soon?' Ali said, 'As soon as they saw us, they surrendered, our reputation has become so widespread that as soon as they saw us, they opened the gates and let us go in'.

I want the commander of the Kookherdi army Commander Hassan to talk to his soldiers and tell them to surrender. Again, what happened next was totally unexpected by Ali or anyone for that matter, as soon as the soldiers in Herang saw Ali and his Black Devils they opened the gates without talking to their Commander Hassan. The soldiers were chanting, 'Ali BinAar—Ali BinAar—Ali BinAar.' Ali was welcomed into the city the same way as he was welcomed in Kookherd. Everyone loved Ali and his Black Devils.

THE BANDITS OF HERANG

Once the Bastaki army entered Herang, the bandits who were living in Herang under the protection of Khan Mirza, closed the walls to their strong hold inside Herang, they also took around 40 hostages. They sent a messenger to Ali that if anything should happen to them or if the Bastaki army would attack the stronghold the hostages will be killed on the spot.

This was the first time Ali had faced a hostage situation and he did not know what to do. So, he met with his team Anwar, Saleh and also Commander Hassan, to seek their advice as to what they should do next. Anwar recommended that they should send someone to negotiate with the bandits so as to know their terms and conditions to free the hostages and leave the city. Ali said, 'The best person I know who could talk to the Bandits is Farhan as he is the man with the Golden Tongue.' Ali asked Farhan to meet with the Bandits and ask for their terms and conditions to surrender.

Farhan went to the gates of the Bandits stronghold under the protection of the Black Devils. Farhan asked to talk with the leader of the bandits. His name was BuNawas, as BuNawas came to the main gate, Farhan asked him what he wanted to do to free the hostages. BuNawas was a very smart man he knew that once he let the hostages go free Ali will take him prisoner and maybe have him killed. So, what to do how to get out of this predicament and not get killed! BuNawas told Farhan to come back after two hours as he needed time to think and consult with his people. He said, 'Don't worry the hostages will be treated well and none of them will be harmed in any way.'

BuNawas met with his people and asked them what to do. They all said that they didn't want to leave, and they loved the city of Herang, and they had their families in Herang, and they didn't want to go and live any place else. So how can we convince Ali BinAar that we want to stay, and we will become law abiding citizens of Herang? BuNawas looked at his men and said, 'How many of you are married with kids?' Around 60 raised their hands so he said to them, 'Would you like to go into business for yourselves? They said, 'Yes, we are not young anymore and this life we are leading is very tiresome and dangerous.' The rest, about 50, were young and had not married yet.

When Farhan came to the gate again after two hours, BuNawas was ready for him. He said to Farhan, 'Please inform Ali BinAar that 60 of us are married and would like to start their own business and live in Herang as merchants, myself and 49 of my men we young, very good fighters and we do not have any family. We would like to join Ali BinAar's Black Devils, we have agreed that we will each take 100 gold coins and the rest of the stolen money will be given to Bayt Al Mall. This will be our repentance for all our crimes, we have only stolen money and goods from caravans, and we have never killed anyone this we swear too, we are not assassins.'

Farhan said, 'I will talk with Ali and get back to you'. Farhan hurried to Ali to tell him what was said. Ali asked Farhan 'You know people better than me do you think he was sincere in what he said. Farhan said 'I am positive that he was very sincere as only a truthful person would be ready to give up so much money. But the thing that surprised me is that he wants to join the Black Devils and not just the army why do you think he asked for that?' Ali said, 'I will meet him and ask him myself as this request really intrigues me also. Why the Black Devils??? I want to know his reasons for joining my elite team'. Ali asked that BuNawas meet with him, BuNawas was now very confident that he would be safe. Agreed to come and meet Ali.

BuNawas opened the gates of the stronghold he and five of his men came out and followed Farhan to meet Ali, it was a strange meeting for Ali, as this was the man who was supposed to kill him, and his family and he is now in front of him. Ali welcomed BuNawas to his majlis. BuNawas said 'I am honoured to meet with the great Ali BinAar. To me you are an amazing man in a few short months you have become a hero of not only BinAar and Bastak, but every person in every city in this province. We all love you and consider you our hero for what you have done for everyone. When Khan Mirza ordered us to attack your caravan, I was not happy. But he was my Khan and I had to obey. I am very happy that things turned out the way it did. Since I sent the message to Farhan informing him of Khan Mirza's dastardly Plan'.

Ali looked at Farhan 'you didn't tell me that BuNawas sent you the information about the attack on our caravan'. Farhan said, 'I wanted you to get the information from him directly as he has been a good friend for many years'. BuNawas said to Ali, 'I was forced into becoming a Bandit but now since I have heard about you and what you and the Khan of Bastak are doing for the people, I wanted to join your army, but I didn't know how, until Khan Mirza gave me the idea'. I would like to inform you that we do not have any hostages. The people you think are our hostages are in fact family members of my men, this was a ploy so that we could get a chance to meet with you'.

Ali said to BuNawas 'You are a very smart man and I agree to all your terms, it will be my honour to have someone like you and your men join the Black Devils. Who better to help me fight Bandits than a person who was a Bandit and who knows all their tactics'. BuNawas said to Ali, 'Believe me, once people will know that we have joined your Black Devils they will come to join you also'. Ali went inside the strong hold and met with all the other Bandits, and they all swore allegiance to Ali and to the Khan of Bastak. The money that was recovered from the stronghold was to be distributed into three parts 50% was distributed among the Bastaki soldiers equally, 20% was sent to the Bayet Al Mall. And 30% was sent to Bastak and BinAar to be distributed among the Merchants who lost their goods when the Bandits attacked their caravans. Each of the Bandits received 100 gold coins as per the agreement so they could start their own business. Ali left Herang and went back to Kookherd to meet with Khan Mohammed on his arrival.

Khan Mohammed arrived the next day from Bastak, he met with Khan Mirza, but this time Khan Mohammed did not just exile him to Bastak. As he was very angry, he exiled Khan Mirza to be taken to the city of Shiraz far away from the

Provence of Hormozgan. As he did not want to see his face ever again to be reminded that this man had once planned the murder of Ali and his family.

Khan Mohammed said to Ali, 'What are you doing my son, I am not a young man, and you are making me travel to different cities every few days. Please give me a rest'. Ali looked at his future father-in-law and said, 'I am sorry for making you travel so much but what to do, the people need to see their new Khan and feel safe that you are now in control of their city'. Khan Mohammed said, 'I know my son, but you also need a rest from all this fighting business, as I was coming in, I saw that the number of your Black Devils had multiplied'. Ali said yes BuNawas and 49 of his men have joined my Black Devils, I am very happy that people are hoping to be members of my team it is an honour for me to get the respect of so many people. Khan Mohammed said, 'now we need to get back and get you married my son'.

Again, Farhan was called to recommend the new mayors of Kookherd and Herang. Farhan smilingly said, 'before the two cities had fallen, I had already found the two perfect candidates to become mayor of the two cities'. Ali and Khan Mohammed met with the two candidates, and they were very satisfied with Farhan's recommendations. The two new mayors were appointed one for Kookherd and the other for Herang and Ali put the new governmental processes in effect, as all the cities under Bastaks' rule should have only one system of government. The system that Ali had put in place was the system created by the Prophet Mohammed Peace be upon him and the Khulafa Al Rasyidin.

Ali and his men left Kookherd and went back to BinAar. Again, Ali's mother was amazed at what keeps happening with her son Ali, and she said, 'We will be leaving in two days so get ready and no more wars for the time being'. Ali responded by saying 'I am sorry mother but this time it was totally out of my control I had to attack them to save everyone's life'. This time Ali did not want to take any chances so when the wedding caravan left BinAar, he took his Black Devils who were now 70 not 20 like before, and the BinAari Cavalry of 400 as protection from any attack on the caravan.

The caravan finally reached Bastak under the protection of the BinAari Cavalry and the Black Devils who have become the most feared warriors in the Province. The people were lined up in the streets of Bastak welcoming Ali BinAar, the hero of the people who has made Bastak into the greatest city in the region that people have started to love and respect. Bastak has now become the center of commerce in the Province, all caravans now have started to come to Bastak first then go to other cities. This has happened in the last few months after the fall of the fortress of BinAar.

The Bastaki method of a wedding is basically comprised of three days of ceremony, these three days usually last around a week with a day of rest between each ceremony. The first ceremony is called 'Akedi or Milcha Ceremony'. This ceremony is the most important part of an Islamic marriage, this event in which the bridegroom and the bride's guardian sign the Islamic marriage contract. After this ceremony the bride and groom are legally married. The second day is called the 'Henna Ceremony' this event is totally for women no men are allowed to attend this ceremony, it is when the bride has Henna drawings put on her hand and feet. The third and last event is called 'Dokhla Wedding Reception'. This event is when the groom's family and the bride's family meet each other. The groom is taken by the bride's father to the women's reception hall to meet his bride and for the brides female family members to meet the groom for the first time, at the of the reception both the bride and groom leave the reception together as husband and wife.

The newly wedded couple stay in the house of the bride, so the family of the bride get to meet the groom. The newlywed couple stay in the bride's parents' house for a minimum of one week to six months or even more. Then the groom takes the Bride to her new home. To live with his parents or her own home. If the bride and groom live in the grooms parents' house, then the house would be large as each family would have a section of the house for themselves. Very similar to the house that Ali lived in with his parents and brothers' families.

Chapter 11

THE WEDDING RECEPTION

The Dokhla Wedding Reception was a very grand affair. It was a wedding that everyone wanted to attend. Not because the Khan of Bastak's daughter was getting married but it was the wedding of Ali BinAar, the hero of the people was getting married, so people from near and far had come to attend the wedding. The reception was split into two receptions, as all Islamic wedding receptions are held separately, one reception was for the Women and the other reception was for the Men.

The Men's reception. Anyone who was anyone had come from faraway cities to attend. It was held in the private garden of the Khan's Palace. To be able to accommodate the number of attendees. BuNawas upon joining the Black Devils made some changes one of the changes was to keep the identity of the Black Devils a secret. So, they had to cover their faces so that only their eyes were visible. The 70 Black Devils had lined up facing each other in a long line in front of the entrance to the reception. All the guests had to walk through the Black Devils to reach the reception area and meet Ali and Khan Mohammed and their close family members, after shaking hands with the wedding party, the guests could then enter the reception area. It was an impressive site as people had heard of the Black Devils and now, they were walking through them to meet Ali BinAar.

Ali's Uncle Marwan, who is now living in Bastak was also present and was a member of the wedding party. He had a brief conversation with Ali and he said 'Ali my dear nephew I knew you had potential as I loved you so much, but I didn't know that you could accomplish so much in such a short time. Never in my dreams could I have ever imagined that one day BinAar, Anveh, Kookherd and Herang would all be part of Bastak! You are amazing. I am sorry I didn't recognize your true potential otherwise we could have done a lot together. Ali said, 'my dear uncle this is the beginning, my dream is much bigger than this and very soon you will see my dream come true by the grace of Allah'.

A large number of Khans, dignitaries and rich merchants had come to the wedding, the largest gathering of such individuals in Bastaks history. They had come not for the wedding but just to get to see the man who may attach their city in the not-so-distant future. As Ali had become so famous that people just opened their gates for him. Is he a Magician? How does he do it? During the evening Khan Farhad of Karmostaj got a chance to meet with Ali privately, Khan Farhad said 'How did you manage to do all what you have done in such a short time?' Ali responded, 'I have done nothing it is only fate that has put me on this course, I am just an instrument that Allah is using to make Bastak the greatest state in the Province.' Khan Farhad asked him I heard that your father gave you 10,000 Gold Dinars and you distributed it all among your solders is that true? Yes, I have all the money I need, and I had no use for the 10,000, so I gave it to those who needed it more than me. Khan Farhad was amazed at this response, he didn't know what to say so he left Ali and joined his party.

After all the guests had arrived dinner was served and it was an amazing sight to see all the large trays of food being brought out and served to the guests, each tray had a stuffed goat lying on a bed of rice. With large bowls of meat or chicken stew. Only two types of drinks are served hot or cold. The hot drink is 'Qahwa' coffee, and cold drinks like Buttermilk or fresh juices like orange, watermelon or lemonade. As all Islamic weddings only in the men's reception, the men start to leave the party after having dinner.

The Women's reception. On the other hand, the woman's reception is another story altogether, no men are allowed to enter the women's reception. The wedding party both the close relatives of the Bride and Groom stand at the entrance to welcome all the guest, in the women's reception they have music singing and dancing. Once all the guests have arrived, dinner is served, the food for both receptions are usually the same. All the women are dressed in their best clothes and jewellery. After dinner, the bride is then brought into the hall, a stage has been erected for her, the stage is approximately 1 meter high and 10 to 15 meters long. The bride is then taken up the stage to sit in the middle of the stage. The ladies then go to the bride and congratulate her, after all the ladies have been given a chance to meet the bride. The groom is then invited to enter the Women's Reception, Khan Mohammed held the right hand of Ali and Prince Abdulla held his left hand and brought him into the hall. Other men are not invited. Before the men could enter the women's section the women are informed so they could cover themselves and put on their veils.

All the women would like to get a closer look at the groom and in this case most women have come to see the famous Ali the hero of BinAar, whom most young girls would love to marry, and here he is, the hero himself for all of the women to see and inspect him closely. As soon as Ali entered the hall all the women started clapping and shouting his name. It was like a celebrity had just walked into the wedding hall. Ali was taken up on the stage and made to sit next to Princess Fatima. Ali was so nervous that he couldn't raise his eyes to see where he was going. That is why every groom needs someone to hold their hands when they enter the wedding hall.

Ali and Princess Fatima were sitting next to each other, and all the relatives of the Bride and Groom were coming on the stage to give their best wishes to the happy couple. Princess Fatima looked at Ali and said, 'Why are you so serious, why don't you smile aren't you happy?' Ali responded by saying 'I would rather be facing an army of 10,000 instead of facing all these women who are really scaring me at the moment'. Princess Fatema laughed and said, 'are you the same Ali whom the Khans are afraid of, fearing a few defenceless women'. Ali responded, 'I can't look at them in the eye, the way they are staring at me, I feel that I am under dressed' and Princess Fatema started laughing and his comment.

After spending almost an hour sitting together Ali and Princess Fatima left the wedding hall as husband and wife, they both went to Princess Fatima's apartments in the palace. As per the traditions in Bastak both families of the bride and groom have a late breakfast with the happy couple, to celebrate the wedding and the joining of both families. This is a very old tradition dating back hundreds of years. The celebrations continued in the palace as with both families having lunch and dinner together, this was to strengthen the bond between families.

The Repercussions of Ali's Actions

The next day Khan Farhad of Karmostaj met with his people and also invited his good friend Khan Adnan of the City of Dashti, to discuss the current situation and what would happen very soon. Khan Farhad said, 'We are one of the closest cities to Bastak, we should expect the army of Bastak under the command of Ali to arrive at our cities very soon, once Ali's army will surround our cities and the soldiers will see Ali on his dancing horse followed by his Black Devils, believe me the soldiers will open the gates and run to welcome Ali and his Black Devils as their saviour, this is what has happened before and trust me it will happen with us. Everyone loves Ali and they will do anything for him'.

Khan Adnan said, 'you are right my friend, did you take a look at those Black Devils with their faces covered standing in line in front of the main entrance, they were really scary. I wouldn't want a fight with them. I have been told that BuNawas the Bandit has joined Ali's Black Devils, so what do you think we should do?' Khan Farhad said, 'That is what I have been thinking about for a few days, and since I had a talk with Ali BinAar in the wedding reception, I am even more afraid of him'. Khan Adnan inquired, 'What do you main after talking with Ali you are even more afraid of him?' Khan Farhad said, 'Ali is one of those people who only thinks about how to help others, he doesn't want money, do you know how much money he gave himself for the capture of each city? It is 100 gold coins, the same as his commanders and nothing else'. Khan Adnan said, 'you must be wrong 100 gold coins per city! That is what I spend in a day'. Khan Farhad said, 'now you understand why I am so sacred of him, what can you do with such a man who doesn't care about money or power, all he cares about is to help people who are suffering, you know I asked him (How did you manage to do all what you have done in such a short time?) Ali responded, (I have done nothing it is only fate that has put me on this course, I am just an instrument that Allah is using to make Bastak the greatest state in the Province.) 'How can you fight someone who thinks he is a hero and will do anything to help the people'.

Khan Adnan said, 'so what do you recommend we do? How can we get out of this situation without losing anything? Do you recommend that we have Ali killed? Or do you have another plan in mind?' Khan Farhad said, 'nothing so drastic my friend, even if we plan to kill him who is the person we could trust to do this dead. I can think of only one thing to do, instead of waiting for Ali to come to us let us join Bastak and change our names from Khan to (El Wally) The Mayor, that way we will be able to manage our own cities, not get exiled to stay in Bastak for the rest of our lives, as what happened to Khan Marwan, Saleem, and Mirza was banished to Shiraz, so what would be our fate, if we defy Ali?'

Khan Farhad continued saying, 'Tomorrow I will request an audience with Khan Mohammed, Ali and the Crown Prince Abdulla, and recommend that our two cities become part of Bastak, what do you say my friend?' Khan Adnan responded, 'if this is what you recommend my friend, then I agree with you as this is the right thing to do, I think this is the best way to keep our cities in our family and keep our wealth without losing anything'. Khan Farhad responded by saying 'now let us sit and put our terms and conditions so that we can put forward our demands, once Khan Mohammed and Ali have agreed to our demands then we can start the merging of our two cities with the Bastaki system of government.

The next morning a messenger from Khan Farhad was sent to request an audience with the top 3 men in Bastak. The audience was granted at the grand majlis of Khan Mohammed, as both Khans entered, they were greeted by Khan Mohammed, Prince Abdulla and Ali, Khan Farhad started the conversation by saying 'I am sure that you all surprised that we have requested this meeting! Let me explain what we have been thinking about ever since the wedding banquet. After seeing what Bastak has achieved in such a short time and after talking with you Ali during the wedding banquet, we have concluded that we should join Bastak in its great vision of unifying all the small cities in this province under one ruler. Karmostaj has a large army of 2,000 infantry and 500 cavalries, Dashti has an army of 1,700 infantry and 350 cavalries, our combined armies will be a great addition to the Bastaki army. Before we join Bastak we have some terms and conditions once agreed to by you than we shall join Bastak and become one state'.

Khan Mohammed was surprised, and he was looking at Ali what do you think, Ali said, 'My dear Khans, this pleases us very much, please tell us your terms and conditions'. Khan Farhad said:

The terms and conditions:

1. Khan Adnan and I shall remain in our cities, and we will govern our cities as the new Mayors of the cities under the Bastaki system of government.
2. Our wealth and properties will remain ours and will not be taken from us.
3. Our children will become Mayer's of the city after our death.
4. Khan Mohammed and Ali BinAar with the Bastaki army will come our cities and inform the people of the new system.
5. The Bandits who are operating from our cities will be asked to leave or go into respectable trade.
6. Ten of our best solders from Karmostaj and 10 soldiers from Dashti will join Ali's Black Devils, this will give our cities prestige that some of our best warriors are a part of the best Bastaki soldiers.

Khan Mohammed said, 'Thank you, my friend for your request, I will let Ali respond to your conditions'. Ali said 'My dear Khan Farhad, I am so happy that you have considered joining Bastak in its great task of unifying the region. Let me address your conditions one by one:

1. Your first condition we agree to without any changes.
2. Your second condition we also agree to without any changes.
3. Your third condition we agree to but with a small change your children must be deserving to become the Mayors of your cities as this job is not a matter of prestige but a responsibility.
4. Your fourth condition we agree to as we would love to visit your two cities.
5. Your fifth condition we agree to, but they will have to surrender the wealth they have stolen from all the merchants and the people, as we did with the Bandits in Herang they can each keep 100 gold dinars to start their own trade.
6. Your sixth condition we agree to, but it is surprising I didn't know that the reputation of the Black Devils was so great that you would be honoured to have 10 of your soldiers join them?

Khan Farhad said, 'we think that your changes to our conditions are fair, now we agree to joining Bastak'. Upon that all the men started embracing each other that it was a great day for Bastak, Karmostaj and Dashti, all these cities had now become one. Khan Mohammed said 'after one week we shall leave Bastak first we will go to Karmostaj as it is closer to Bastak, and we will be your gusts Khan Farhad for three days then we shall go to Dashti and be your guests Khan Adnan for three days, I hope that is agreeable to you both as I do not wish that our friendship be endangered by any ill feeling to arise between us now or in any time in the future, we are friends and we will always be friends no matter what'.

As soon as the meeting had finished Ali went directly to meet his wife Princess Fatima and tell her the good news, as soon as he informed her of what happened she said, 'again you will leave me alone and go traveling with my father having fun and leaving me hear alone with no one to talk to'. Ali said, 'Who told you I will leave you alone, you will come with me, don't you want to visit Karmostaj and Dashti?' Princess Fatima said, I would love to come with you, as I have never seen these two cities before.'

The preparations for visiting the two cities had started and everyone was so excited at the news that cities had started to join Bastak of their own accord. Ali started thinking to be fair to all the member cities, each city should have a 10-men representation in the Black Devils. So, during this week the city of Bastak, Anveh, Kookherd and Herang were informed, and 10 men were chosen from their cities as the city of BinAar had a 20 men represented in the Black Devils. Suddenly, the number of men in the Black Devils had risen from 70 men to 110 men and they were all cavalries with Black horses, all men had their face covered with only their eyes visible.

On the appointed day, an army of 2,000 cavalries left Bastak and reached Karmostaj the next day, once the army arrived all the people of Karmostaj came out of the city to greet the Khan of Bastak and to catch a glimpse of Ali BinAar the Hero of Hormozgan. The view from the walls of Karmostaj was amazing, the Bastaki cavalries was dressed in white with steel breast plates and Ali in front of the army with his Black Devils, the people were shouting the names of the Khan and Ali in the streets. It was an amazing spectacle that everyone was enjoying this great celebration of the joining of the two cities under the rule of Khan Mohammed who is the legitimate ruler of the province of Hormozgan. It was amazing, the people were so excited on this glorious day of celebrations all the shops and markets were closed people were having a great time as they could see a brighter future for them and their children. The procession continued from the entrance of the city all the way to the palace with the people throwing flowers at the soldiers. It was strange for Princess Fatima to see all the girls scream Ali's name as soon as they saw him in the procession, this was something she did not expect, that the girls were in-love with her husband.

As the procession arrived at the Palace, they all went to the balcony and Khan Mohammed addressed the crowd of people who had gathered in front of the palace, informing them of the changes. The people of Karmostaj were ecstatic after hearing the wonderful news, they are now a part of Bastak and Ali BinAar is now their protector. That evening Princess Fatima said to Ali, 'It seems like the people love you more than my father'. Ali said, 'That is not true they all love your father, but young people are sometimes strange they like to idolize young people like themselves'. Princess Fatima responded, 'Do you think only young people do that I saw some old people also shouting your name'. Ali said, 'That may be true but that does not mean that they love your father any less. Your father is a great man he is my mentor and I owe him everything'.

The next morning Ali took Princess Fatima to the marketplace as she needed to see the city, the people surrounded them just wanting to shake Ali's hand. As Princess Fatima looked on, she started to truly understand that her husband is no ordinary man, the people would not love him so much if they did not feel that he loved them more than they loved him. You could see it in their eyes, the admiration, love, and respect they have for Ali makes him an extraordinary man, such a man would sacrifice anything to help the people. Now she started to worry that if she does not take care of him there are thousands who would gladly take her place and do anything for Ali.

After spending three days in Karmostaj they all left to visit Dashti, this time the cavalries increased to 2,500 and the Black Devils increased to 120. They reached the city of Dashti the next day. Again, the people of Dashti had come out of the city to welcome Khan Mohammed and see the great Ali BinAar with his dancing horse people just loved the great spectacle just looking at all the cavalries in white and headed by the Black devils. A beautiful site to see as 2,500 cavalries, no one has an army of that size anywhere in the province, and now soon to be 2,850 cavalries with the 350 from Dashti. Just like what happened in Karmostaj, all the shops and markets were closed, people were celebrating in the streets, the people were shouting the names of the Khan and Ali's in the streets.

After the procession reached the palace and the Khan talked with the people from the balcony of the palace, Khan Mohammed asked to meet with Ali and Princess Fatima, in his private quarters in the gust palace. Khan Mohammed said, 'Ali since the moment I met you 9 months ago, my life has changed forever, could you please give me a rest, I am not as young as I used to be and I have been traveling nonstop for the past three months from one city to another city, I never thought I would ever visit these cities and now they belong to me, all because of you my son, but please stop, give me some rest'. Princess Fatima said to her father, 'Isn't this what you always wanted father?' Khan Mohammed said, 'Yes, it was always my dream, but things are happening so fast I don't know how to handle this. As of now, I have seven cities and their surrounding towns with more than 10,000 infantry and 3,000 cavalry and I am sure that it will double very soon. When will this stop my son?'

Ali smiled and said, 'My dear Khan, it is my first duty to protect you and look after your health, so from now on I will take Prince Abdulla with me to all the new cities, I hope you agree to this as he is the next Khan of Bastak. Princess Fatima said 'yes father this is the right thing to do let my brother Abdulla go with Ali and you can rest in Bastak and when you feel relaxed then you can go on a tour of the cities and take me with you as it is very tiring to travel with the army from place to place. It is much better to travel in a caravan'. Khan Mohammed agreed that from now on Prince Abdulla will be travelling with the army from city to city.

After Ali had so much experience with so many new cities, he started taking with him the government officials to train the government employees in the new cities that are joining Bastak on the new government practices and processes of Bastak. Ali recommended to Khan Mohammed that each city should only have 1,000 infantries only and the cavalries from each city will join the Bastaki Cavalries. This will reduce costs and a large infantry is unnecessary as no city in the province has an infantry of more than 1,000 men. But having a large cavalry makes any army very powerful as speed is very important in any war. This was agreed to by Khan Mohammed and Prince Abdulla, as he left all the military decisions with Ali.

Without planning, without expecting Ali BinAar had become the most powerful man in the Provence. To the people his name was synonymous with saviour, Hero of the people. The Khans feared him as they knew they could not face him in battle, and the Bandits hated him and prayed for his death as he had put a stop to all their activities in a matter of a few months, they had become so afraid of Ali that they were to sacred of attacking any caravan that Ali may appear and destroy them.

It was amazing people started to feel safe that a person named Ali BinAar was protecting them, they did not fear going out of the city to another city as they knew that bandits did not have the guts to attack anyone, as Ali BinAar would come and punish them. People started making stories about Ali, some true and some completely untrue, as people have a habit of talking if they do not have anything to say they make up a story.

Chapter 12

THE NEW CITIES JOINING BASTAK

The Khans had heard of what happened with Karmostaj, Dashti and all the other cities in the province that had joined Bastak, they started sending their emissaries to join Bastak exactly like Karmostaj and Dashti, they all had the same terms and conditions that Khan Farhad had put forward to the Khan of Bastak. Over the next two years many cities started joining the Bastaki alliance of cities. Emissaries from Dideban, Kuhij, Mistan, Janah, Daarbast, Kemeshk, Bochir, Gauberi, Heshniz, Behdeh, Charak, and two port cities had joined the alliance like Bandar-e-Mogham, and Bandar-e-Divan. The Bastak alliance had grown to 20 cities. This was an amazing accomplishment in a 3-year period.

Ali and his wife Princess Fatima had a large house built for them near the palace of Khan Mohammed, the house was very large with eight 3-bedroom apartments on the upper floor the ground floor had two grand Majlises and two guest apartments for when Ali's family came to visit. Ali and Fatima had a son and they named him Mohammed Bin Ali; it was a happy time for everyone in the province, as the fighting between all the warring cities had ended, the Bandit problem was over, the caravans were safe to go from one city to the next, without being attacked by Bandits. The prices of goods had come down as merchants did not have to increase their prices to cover security costs or to recover the costs of goods stolen by Bandits.

In 1778, a group of bandits attacked a caravan going from the city of Kemeshk to the city of Bochir, both cities were in the Bastaki alliance of cities. When the news reached Ali, he was enraged that after two years of peace in the province suddenly they had a Bandit attack on a caravan under the protection of Bastak. Ali immediately called Farhan and Asem to discover who was behind the Bandit attack, Ali said 'please find out which city was harbouring the Bandits who had the audacity to attack a caravan under the protection of Bastak, this is something Bastak will never forgive they have to pay and the Khan who is protecting them will have to answer to Bastak for allowing this to happen'. Asem said 'I will go to the cities that are near Kemeshk and Bochir who are not a part of the alliance and find the culprits'. Farhan said I will start communicating with all my contacts in that region to find the Bandits and where they came from'.

Ali met with Khan Mohammed, Prince Abdulla and the war council members Anwar, Saleh, The Bastak Garrison Commander Zain-Ul-Abideen, and Farhan. Ali said to the Khan 'We have to respond to this aggression without any delay, if we do nothing other Bandits will start attacking our caravans and all our hard work would have been for nothing. This is a time to show strength, and I will call our soldiers from all the alliance cities to each city to provide 500 infantries Bastak had 5000 cavalries stationed in Bastak and 260 Black Devils. The remainder of the Garrison will remain in the cities for protection. The soldiers will start assembling outside the gates of Bastak, once we know the name of the city harbouring the Bandits the army will leave to confront them'. Ali continued saying 'my dear Khan, I hope you agree with the plan?' Khan Mohammed said, 'the plan looks good, but don't you think we should contact the Khan first before we send our army?' Prince Abdulla said, 'Father I think we should send the army as soon as we can they started this and it was not us so we should not give them a chance to do it again'.

The discussions continued some agreed with Ali and some agreed with the Khan, finally Ali said, 'it has been decided that once we find out which city is responsible for this aggression, we will send a messenger to ascertain what happened and why. Once we get the response, we will decide what we will do next, but we should gather the army just in case we have to go to war'. Khan Mohammed said this is good, we should at least give a chance to the Khan responsible to give us their excuse for this unprovoked aggression'.

Six days after the incident Asem sent a courier pigeon with the information with the name of the culprit city, the message read 'the city of Ashkenan with 137 bandits', the distance from Bastak to Ashkenan was approximately 107 km. This distance could be covered by an army in approximately three to four days. As the infantry needed to walk that distance travelling for 11 to 12 hours per day. The city of Ashkenan as per the current maps is in Faris Province, Ashkenan was a part of the Zand Dynasty with the capital in Shiraz.

As per the agreement during the Bastak war council meeting, a messenger was sent to Khan Reza of Ashkenan, demanding retribution for this atrocity against the Bastaki Alliance. The messenger who was sent, his name was Adam bin Abdulla, he was from the city of Kookherd a trusted member of the Black Devils, he reached Ashkenan within two days of travelling, upon reaching Ashkenan it was during the evening time before sunset, he requested an audience with Kan Reza, upon entering the grand majlis Adam said 'I am a messenger from Khan Mohammed of Bastak and this is a letter from him to you', he delivered the letter and awaited the response. Khan Reza opened the letter and read its contents.

('In the name of Allah, the Most Gracious, the Most Merciful')

To Khan Reza from Khan Mohammed,

We have been informed that the Bandits who attacked one of our caravans during the past week are under the protection of Ashkenan, we request that you hand the Bandits over to the Bastaki Alliance and have them return the goods stolen from the Caravan and pledge never to attack any caravan under the protection of the Bastaki Alliance.

Khan Mohammed of Bastak.')

As soon as Khan Reza read the letter, he was so enraged that he ordered the execution of Adam the messenger. Khan Reza said, 'who does Khan Mohammed think he is, he cannot order me and hope that I will obey. I will show him who Khan Reza is and what I can do. Execute the messenger and send his head to Khan Mohammed with my letter'.

Three days later a messenger from Ashkenan arrived in Bastak and asked for an audience with Khan Mohammed, immediately the War Council was called to gather in the Grand Majlis. As the messenger entered Ali was surprised as 'he was wondering where Adam the messenger he sent to Ashkenan was?' The letter was delivered to Khan Mohammed, and it was read out aloud to everyone.

(From Khan Reza to Khan Mohammed,

How dare you send a letter to me demanding that I give you the Bandits! My city is not a small city without any protection, we are Ashkenan under the protection of the Zand Dynasty and we fear no one. Find my response in the box sent with my messenger.

Khan Reza of Ashkenan.')

When the box was opened, they found the severed head of the messenger Adam inside. Everyone in the majlis was extremely enraged as this was not done. A messenger is respected by everyone and killing a messenger is considered to be the most heinous crime committed by any person. Ali was so enraged he gave the order that the army should be ready to move against Ashkenan the next day, and all the soldiers should be informed of what has just happened and that Khan Reza is the person that should be executed for this terrible crime. Ali also ordered that the oldest son of Adam should come with them to Ashkenan to avenge the death of his father Adam.

Ali left the Grand Majlis and went back home, when Princess Fatima saw him, she immediately knew that something was wrong. Ali was so enraged that he was finding it very difficult to breathe, she started whipping his face and hands with cold water, just so he could calm down, he was unable to express why he was so angry. She called her lady in waiting Anwar's wife to find out what happened, she ran to see her husband, and Anwar told her what happened, she went back to Princess Fatima and informed her why Ali was so angry. She was finally able to help Ali calm down and he fell asleep.

Ali never knew that anyone could be so ruthless as to kill a messenger whose job is to deliver information from one place to another, Ali always had a great respect for messengers and to have one executed is a taboo and act of savagery and barbarism.

THE BASTAK, ASHKENAN WAR

Ali with Prince Abdulla, Anwar, Saleh, and Farhan all left Bastak with the army 12,000 infantry, 5,000 cavalries, and 12 cannons to attack Ashkenan. Asem had already infiltrated the City of Ashkenan and gathered information about the city walls and its defensive capabilities. Farhan was sent ahead to work with Asem and spy on the city from within. It took the Bastaki army 4 days to reach Ashkenan, Asem sent a messenger to Ali with the city's defensive capabilities.

Ashkenan had three great walls. At the back of the city was a high mountain, the city had two walls, an inner wall, and an outer wall. The distance between both walls was 50 m. The city had three main gates, one on every wall. The city had 12 cannons, 4 cannons on every wall. The strength of the army was 2,000 infantry and 500 cavalries. As per the information sent by Asem. The cannons on the left wall were old and smaller than the cannons on the front wall. The fire power of the cannons on the left wall were much less than normal cannons. Ali knew what was to be done so the plan was put in place.

The next day the Bastaki army arrived at Ashkenan and took up positions out of range of the cannons. The Bastaki army was divided into three parts, main entrance 4,000 infantry and 2,000 cavalries, right and left walls 4,000 infantry and 1,500 cavalry each, with all 12 cannons on the left wall as soon as the cannons where in place the bombardment of the left wall started. As the old cannons of the left wall did not have the strength to reach the Bastaki cannons, they were destroyed during the first hour, and the bombardment continued, the Ashkenan's army stood hopeless looking at the bombardment of the wall as they couldn't move the other cannons to protect the left wall. The bombardment of the outer wall continued during the night at about midnight, a large portion of the left wall had collapsed, the cannons were moved a little closer and the bombardment of the inner wall started.

The soldiers were wondering why the infantry did not attack the breach in the wall. Anwar and Saleh both came to Ali in the night and asked him why the infantry was not ordered to attack, as they had the element of darkness, and they could start climbing the inner wall. Ali said, 'be patient I have something else in mind a war of nerves', Saleh asked 'what do you mean war of nerves', Ali said 'currently Farhan and Asem are inside the city telling people to open the gates and let us in peacefully and if the army entered by force than they may lose all they have'. Anwar said, 'that is a very devious plan do you think it will work?' Ali said, 'if I know Farhan and Asem they can do it, they will make the people see the logic behind welcoming us as their saviours instead of forcing us to enter the city with full force'.

The next morning a large part of the inner wall had collapsed, and the army awaited to be given the command to attack the city but still nothing, suddenly the main gates of the front wall were opened, and the people rushed out to welcome the Bastaki army into the city. As soon as the gates were opened, Ali sent a carrier pigeon to Princess Fatima informing her that the city had been liberated. (When Ali was leaving Bastak Princess Fatima knew that Ali was very angry, and she told him to think carefully before doing anything rash that could end badly for him and the army. So, she asked him to send her a message when the city was liberated, and that is what Ali did before he entered the city.)

Before Ali entered the city of Ashkenan he sent a force of 500 infantry to take control of the palace and take Khan Reza into custody, this was to be done before Prince Abdulla was to arrive at the palace. Ali's exact command was 'as soon as you see Khan Reza, take him into custody, and put him in chains, when we see Khan Reza, we want to see him in chains. This man does not deserve anyone's respect as he is a messenger killer so treat him accordingly'. Prince Abdulla said to Ali, 'Be reasonable brother; don't let this effect you so much', Ali said 'Sorry brother that you are disturbed by my actions, but some actions are unforgivable and, in my eyes, killing a messenger is unforgivable. But you represent the Khan, so you have the right to change my orders as you see fit'. Prince Abdulla said, 'Your orders are fine, but you shouldn't make such a big thing out of it'. Ali said 'I don't like Tyrants I never did, and Khan Reza is an evil tyrant, I have made it my life's mission to stand up to tyrants were ever they may be. My uncle Marwan was a tyrant and I had to fight him also'. Prince Abdulla said, 'you are right and that is exactly why we are here'.

Ali and Prince Abdulla entered the city of Ashkenan on the head of the army, The Black Devils 100 were riding in front of Prince Abdulla and Ali and 169 behind them after them came the cavalry and then the infantry, it was a long procession more than 12,000 soldiers were moving as one, Ali left a large number of soldiers outside the city to protect the Bastaki Camp and the weapons, this was normal practice, not all the soldiers would enter the liberated city, as the procession moved towards the palace the people were shouting the name of Prince Abdulla and Ali all along the streets until they reached the palace, Ashkenan was a large city with more than 15,000 inhabitants.

When the procession reached the palace Prince Abdulla and Ali whet to the palace balcony to talk to the people, as the people were celebrating the arrival of the Bastaki army to liberate them from Khan Reza and his bandits. After that they went to the grand majlis, and Prince Abdulla gave the command to bring Khan Reza to the majlis. Within a short period of time Khan Reza was brought into the majlis in shackles. Prince Abdulla looked at him and said, 'This is the consequence of your actions. What did you think was going to happen when you killed the messenger, did you think that nothing will happen and Bastak will be so afraid of you that we will do nothing?' Khan Reza said, 'I am Khan Reza, and you have no right to attack Ashkenan, we are a part of the Zand Dynasty, and you all will pay for this transgression against a mighty dynasty'. Ali got angry again and said, 'You are a disgraceful Khan, and you should never have been made Khan of such a great city, if your Zand Dynasty is so great and they will protect you, why are you in chains and on your knees in front of us?' Ali said to the guards, 'Bring Adam's son to the majlis and let him decide the fate of this person, whom I do not wish to see ever again'.

Suddenly a young boy walked into the majlis, Ali asked him, 'are you the son of Adam?' the boy said 'yes, he is my father'. Ali said, 'What is your name?' the boy responded, 'My name is Omran'. Ali said to Omran, 'You are responsible to avenge your father's death, and here is the person who killed your father, it is your right to ask for justice, what do you say my boy'. Suddenly Khan Reza shouted, 'before you decide, I will pay you 10,000 gold coins as blood money, please forgive me for killing your father'. Khan Reza's minsters started talking with the boy to convince him to take the money. One minister said, 'take the money my boy, remember you have to take care of your mother and little brothers and sisters, how will you live, take the money'.

The boy started thinking about his family and what would happen to them. Farhan looked at Omran and said to him, 'Do not worry about your family, the government of Bastak will take care of you and your family, as your father was killed in the line of duty. Just kill him and I will make sure you are taken care of'. Omran looked at Ali and said to him, 'I respect you and your advice, my father loved you more than anyone, he once told me that if anything should happen to him, I should come to you if I needed anything, what do you think I should do?' Ali looked at Omran and said, 'your father was right, and I will always be here for you and your family, my advice is to take the 10,000 gold coins as this will be more than enough for you to take care of your family and never need to ask anyone for anything'. Omran said to Prince Abdulla, 'I will take the blood money and I forgive him'.

Prince Abdulla said to the guards 'Please remove his chains and let him go free'. When the chains were removed, Khan Reza said, 'wait and see I had sent a messenger to Shiraz informing them that you will be attacking soon, and an army from Shiraz would be on its way to destroy you and your army very soon'. Price Abdulla said, 'remove him from the majlis'. Then he looked at Ali and said, 'I was amazed at what you said to Omran', Ali said, 'The boy asked for my advice, and I couldn't give him bad advice even though I wanted Reza dead so much, it was better for the boy and his family to take the money, I had to leave my personal feelings aside and think of the boy first'. Prince Abdulla said, 'you are amazing I thought you would tell him to have Reza executed, as I knew how much you hated him'. Ali said, 'I hated him yes, but I loved Omran and his family more'.

Now fate makes a move, as Khan Reza was living the palace, with his family, the people had heard that he was pardoned by the son of the messenger, but many people still hated him for what he had done to them for many years, so as soon as he was out in the open with no guards protecting him 10 men actually ran towards him and knifed him to death before anyone could stop them. This was the fate of a tyrant who mistreated his own people, they took the law into their own hands and avenged themselves upon him.

THE ASHKENAN BANDITS

After all the important matters were taken care of, it was time to take care of the Bandits the Cause of all these problems, the leader of the Bandits name was Asad' Allah, he had 137 Bandits working with him, a very dangerous number of very experienced guerrilla fighters. BuNawas knew Asad' Allah, as he had met him a few times, BuNawas recommended that he meet with Asad' Allah and convince him to surrender, Ali agreed to this proposal. BuNawas went to the Bandits strong hold with 20 men and asked to meet with Asad' Allah, he was granted entrance.

When BuNawas entered the majlis of Asad' Allah, he was a bit surprised as it looked just like the majlis of the Khan of Bastak, Asad' Allah said to BuNawas, 'Welcome my friend how are you it has been 4 years since I saw you last', BuNawas said, 'Yes my friend it has been a long time, I am a bit surprised to that your majlis looks like the majlis of the Khan of Bastak', Asad Allah, laughed and said, 'You are right my friend before I had chairs but since I heard of the Khan of Bastak and Ali BinAar and you joined the army of Ali the Black Devils I have been trying to copy what they have been doing'. BuNawas said, 'I am a bit surprised my friend since you have been copying what they have been doing, then why did you attack the caravan that was under the Bastaki Alliances protection?'

Asad' Allah said, 'let me tell you the full story of what happened, after three years of Bastaki expansion that has grown into 20 cities, Khan Reza called me to his Palace, I was surprised that he called me, we usually just sent him his share of the profits from our attacks, but for him to call me to the palace was a first for me.' BuNawas said he called you?' Asad' Allah said 'Yes, my friend, when I met Khan Reza he said, I want you to attack a caravan under the protection of the Bastaki Alliance, I asked him why? He said I want to destroy Bastak, and everything connected with it, as they have grown to become a very powerful Alliance and if I don't put a stop to it now, they may come for Ashkenan and me very soon'. BuNawas said, 'so it was Khan Reza who planned the attack on the caravan!' Asad' Allah continued saying, 'I asked Khan Reza how will the attack on the caravan destroy the expansion of the Bastaki Alliance? Khan Reza said, since we are under the direct control of Shiraz, the capital of the Zand Dynasty any attack on us will be considered a direct attack on the Zand Dynasty, that means Shiraz will send an army to destroy Bastak and its Alliance forever'.

BuNawas said, 'This is an amazing plan by Khan Reza. So, what happened next?' Asad' Allah said, 'Khan Reza ordered me to attack the caravan and kill everyone in the caravan to really anger the Khan of Bastak so that he would launch an attack on Ashkenan, then he would be able to call for help from Shiraz to save the city from the Bastaki army.' BuNawas said, 'But you didn't kill anyone in the caravan', Asad' Allah said, I am not a killer yes, I am a thief but Neither me nor any of my men has killed anyone. We attacked the caravan as per Khan Reza's instructions, but we only took the merchandise, we didn't kill anyone. But when Khan Reza got the news that we didn't kill anyone he was very angry with us, and he promised to take revenge on us for not following his orders'. BuNawas said, 'Now it makes sense why no one was killed in the caravan, so what happened next?'. Asad' Allah said, 'when the Khan of Bastak sent the messenger to Khan Reza, it was his chance to make Bastak very angry and attack Ashkenan. So, he killed the messenger to force Bastak to attack, now you know the full story of what happened'.

BuNawas said, 'Khan Reza was an evil man to have made such a dastardly plan to make people do exactly like he wanted,' Asad' Allah said, 'But with all his planning he didn't take into account the one person who could destroy all his plans and that is Ali BinAar, he thought that once Bastak would attack, the walls of Ashkenan would protect it from the invading army until the Zand army would arrive and defeat them. He didn't think that the walls of Ashkenan would fall so fast and the city would surrender after one day of siege. He didn't consider that Ali BinAar was a great general and an expert tactician, so all his plans were destroyed in just one day, but he sent a message to Shiraz for help and the army will be coming soon you may have 5 or 6 days before the Zand army arrives'.

BuNawas said, 'So, my friend what are your terms to surrender', Asad' Allah said, 'I have 90 men who have been waiting to join the Black Devils for two years and the rest have families and they would like to go into respectable trade. We want the same conditions as you had when you joined the Black Devils, you can take all the money and merchandise that we have taken over the years and give each of us just 100 gold dinars, will Ali BinAar agree to these teams?'

BuNawas said, 'Ali would be very happy and honoured to have you and your men join his Black Devils, I want you to come with me and tell Prince Abdulla and Ali the full story as you told me, and then I would like you to ask Prince Abdulla to agree to your terms, once he will agree to all your terms and conditions and I know he will, Ali will gladly agree that you join his men,'. BuNawas and Asad' Allah went together to meet Prince Abdulla and Ali, after informing them of Khan Reza's plan to destroy Bastak, they finally understood what happened and why it happened. Prince Abdulla agreed to all of Asad' Allah's terms and conditions, and Ali was happy with the addition to his Black Devils. Suddenly the Black Devils grew to 350 with the addition of 90 from the Ashkenan and the youngest member Omran son of Adam the youngest Black Devil.

Now Ali had to start preparing for the arrival of the Zand army from Shiraz, as per the information from Asad' Allah, the army should arrive in 5 or 6 days.

Chapter 13

THE BASTAK SHIRAZ WAR

The city of Shiraz is an old city; it was built around 2000 BC. Over the years many dynasties have occupied Shiraz, it was a part of the Persian empire until it was conquered by Saad Ibn Abi Waqqas, AD 651. Later in AD 1280, Shiraz was saved from the Mongol invasion by the diplomacy of Abu Bakr ibn Saad a local Attabak. Genghis Khan was so enamoured by the ruler of Shiraz that he named him Kutlug Khan and considered him as a friend.

In AD 1387, Shiraz was occupied by Timur Lung or Tamerlane as he is known, Tamerlane was a Turco-Mongol conqueror who founded the Timurid Empire in and around modern-day Afghanistan, Iran, and Central Asia, he become the first ruler of the Timurid dynasty. He is widely regarded as one of the greatest military leaders and tacticians in history, as well as one of the most brutal. He made Shiraz his capital city and brought Shiraz back its former glory.

In 1744, Nader Shah of the Afsharid Dynasty captured the city of Shiraz. A large section of the city was destroyed during the war. From AD 1747 to AD 1800, a three-way power struggle in Iran continued between the Afsharid Dynasty, the Zand Dynasty, and the Qajar Dynasty In AD 1750. Karim Khan Zand moves to Shiraz and takes the title of People's Representative, (Vakil-Ol-Roaya). He established the Zand Dynasty, with Shiraz as its capital. The City of Shiraz is rebuilt again. It was Structured into 11 quarters (10 Muslim and one Jewish). A Huge moat and wall surrounding the city, with six gates. Culture, Arts, and minorities flourished during this time, under the Zand Dynasty.

The City of Ashkenan was under the Zand Dynasty so when Khan Reza was informed that the Bastaki army was on its way to Ashkenan, he sent a messenger to Shiraz asking for help. As Khan Reza boasted and threatened Prince Abdulla and Ali that the Zand army was on its way. So now Ali had to create a plan for how to defeat the Zand army. The distance between Shiraz and Ashkenan was about 450 km. The distance could be covered in about 9 to 10 days depending on the speed of the army. As a large portion of the walls of Ashkenan had collapsed, this meant that the city could not be protected, so the citizens of Ashkenan were not safe if the Zand army entered the city, they may pillage and destroy the city of Ashkenan and Ali has to save the city from anybody who may hurt the people of Ashkenan as they were now his responsibility.

Ali started looking for a good location that would put the Bastaki army between The Zand army and the city of Ashkenan. Ali found a nice hill that blocked the way of the Zand army, a small pass between the hill and a mountain was the only pass to reach Ashkenan from Shiraz. So, Ali sent the army to occupy the hill and fortify the hill from any invading army. Ali put his plans in place for the fortification of the hill to be finished in five days. Ali lined all the cannons on the hill including the eight cannons from Ashkenan, a total of 16 cannons. He put 8,000 infantry on the hill and divided the 5,500 cavalry and 4,000 infantry into two parts as the valley in front of the hill was surrounded by trees on both sides so half of the army was hidden in the trees on the right and the other half of the army was on hidden in the trees on the left, so when the Zand army attacked the army on the hill the other two armies would close in on the Zand army in an Envelopment military tactic by exploiting the enemies flank, and blocking the enemies retreat and reducing the casualties. This was the plan that Ali put in place.

After six days, the Zend army finally arrived at the planned location. The Zand army had a strength of 18,000 infantry, 2.000 cavalries and 6 cannons. The army was commanded by a veteran commander called Zaki Khan. As soon as Zaki Khan arrived, he found that he was facing a small army of 8,000 infantry and 350 cavalries. This made him feel more arrogant, so, he asked to meet with the commander of the Bastaki army. When Ali received the messenger from Zaki

Khan to meet him he was so excited to meet Zaki Khan, the famous undefeated commander of the Zand army who was now facing him in battle. Ali came down from the hill with BuNawas and Asad' Allah and 20 Black Devils.

When Zaki Khan saw Ali, he started laughing, 'you are the commander of the Bastaki army?' Ali said, 'yes I am', Zaki Khan said 'you are a child!', Ali said 'I maybe young but I am a match for you any time'. Zaki Khan said, 'boy you have no idea what I am capable of', Ali said 'it doesn't matter what you are capable of, the main thing is who is victorious in the end'. Zaki Khan said, 'You are right boy, but I have destroyed armies much bigger than yours during my career, that is why I am in command of the Zand army'. Ali said 'I am happy for you but remember if you win it will not be a big achievement, but if I win, it will be the greatest achievement in my life, as I would have defeated Zaki Khan the commander of the Zand army. A boy 21 years old'. Zaki Khan said to Ali, 'I must say you are a brave boy so let me give you a piece of advice surrender and I will let you live; fight and I will be forced to kill you and everyone in your army, I like your hours I will take it for my own'. Ali said to Zaki Khan, 'My dear Commander Zaki Khan, I have some sad news for you, this will be your first defeat and at the hands of a Boy as you call me. so, show me how good a commander you are, and I will show you how good a tactician I am. Remember after your defeat I will not kill everyone in your army I will just take you all as prisoners, this is what we call Bastaki mercy?'

Ali left Zaki Khan and went back to the top of the hill and gave the command for the cannons to start firing, as he did not want to give Zaki Khan a chance to think about what he would do next. And after speaking with Zaki Khan, he lost all respect for the arrogant man. Zaki Khan on the other hand gave the command for the Zand cannons to start firing. But instead of firing cannonballs. They started firing metal stars with four pointed edges one inch in diameter. Each blast hurled 100 metal stars, with the first volley many Bastaki solders got injured. Including Ali got a metal star in his left shoulder. Ali was surprised he had never seen anything like this before. He ordered his men to protect themselves with shields. Ali immediately gave orders to destroy the Zand cannons before they could hurt more of his soldiers. With 16 cannons, Ali was able to take out the Zand cannons in no time at all.

As soon as the cannons were taken out Ali gave the command to give a frontal attack, so the soldiers from the hill start the descent, the Zand soldiers were concentrating on the descending army, they didn't see the Bastaki army attack from the right and left cutting of the flank of the Zand army, within minutes the Zand army were surrounded by the Bastaki army. It was a swift attack. That Zaki Khan didn't expect from a backward army that in his eyes were inexperienced in war. Zaki Khan and his officers, and almost all the Zand army were all taken prisoner. The Zand army suffered about 150 dead with 350 injured, the Bastaki army had only 23 dead and 120 injured. The battle lasted approximately 2.5 hours. It was over before noon, a surprising short time for such an epic battle that its repercussions would last for more than 140 years to come.

After the battle Zaki Khan and his officers were taken to Ashkenan to meet with Prince Abdulla, and Ali, as Zaki Khan and his offices were brought into the grand majlis they had to walk through the line of the Black Devils. In the Grand majlis were Prince Abdulla, Ali, Anwar, Saleh, BuNawas and Asad' Allah were waiting to receive them. Prince Abdulla welcomed Zaki Khan and said, 'Welcome General Zaki Khan it is an honour to meet you, I have heard a lot about your exploits', Zaki Khan said, 'the sad thing is that I didn't hear anything about the exploits of Ali BinAar, if I had I would have been better prepared, when I met you Ali, I felt insulted that Bastak had sent you to fight with me a proven commander who had never lost a battle in 15 years'. Ali smiled and said, 'you were defeated by your own arrogance as you didn't see half my army that was hiding on both sides of your army, that was your first mistake, your second mistake was you underestimated me by thinking I was a small boy'.

BuNawas said, 'I have been with Ali for more than two years and I have never seen anyone who could plan a battle better than he could. You were defeated before the battle had even started my dear general Zaki Khan'. Asad' Allah said, 'I have been dreaming of joining the Black Devils ever since my friend BuNawas joined more than two years ago, and thanks to Khan Reza with his stupid plan to destroy Bastak and the Bastaki Alliance, he managed not only to destroy Ashkenan and hand the city over to Bastak, but also, he had the fierce Zand army defeated at the hands of the Bastaki army'. Zaki Khan said, 'so what do you plan to do with us now'. Ali said, 'we plan to negotiate a peace treaty Between Bastak and the Zand Dynasty, the treaty will not only benefit the Zand Dynasty but also the Bastaki Alliance of cities for many years to come'. Prince Abdulla said, 'I will contact my father Khan Mohammed and ask him to come to Ashkenan, so that we could negotiate and agree on a peace treaty that would be beneficial for all parties involved'.

THE BASTAK SHIRAZ PEACE TREATY

A courier Pigeon was sent to Khan Mohamed requesting his presence in Ashkenan, Khan Mohammed arrived after 4 days of travelling, Ali got a surprise that Princess Fatima and their son had also joined Khan Mohammed.

When Ali saw Princess Fatima, he asked her 'why did you come on this trip, Mohammed is still young, and it would have been a difficult trip for him'. Princess Fatima said, 'Don't worry I am with him, and everything is fine, you don't have to worry about our son'. Ali said I didn't mean that; I was just worried about you and him'. Princess Fatima said, 'Don't worry, we are fine, and I wanted to see my husband after I heard that you got injured'. Ali said, 'I am fine I got one of those metal stars in my left shoulder from one of those cannons that we managed to destroy'.

Princess Fatima looked at Ali's shoulder and said, 'you men never think what happens to us women when you get injured in battle, and then you calmly say that My son is too young to travel, if this war was not important I would never have let you go'.

Later that day Zaki Khan was presented to Khan Mohammed, and they talked about the current situation and the need for a treaty that would benefit all parties. Zaki Khan said to Khan Mohammed, 'I congratulate you on choosing a great commander like Ali to lead your army. I have never met anyone like him in battle, I have been fighting as a commander for more than 15 years and losing a battle before it actually started was an amazing feat by any standards'. Khan Mohammed said, 'At least you managed to fight a little, he never even gave me that chance, the night before the battle started, he took me prisoner in my tent when I was sleeping'. Zaki Khan said, 'I can't believe this'.

Khan Mohammed said, 'We were going to start the battle in the morning with the fortress of BinAar, and I said to my men, 'I will go to sleep so that I could wake up early and get everything ready for the coming siege', during the night I was awakened by Ali with his sword on my chest. Ever since that time, I knew that Ali was an amazing warrior, and I couldn't wait for him to join my army'. Zaki Khan said, 'at first, I felt insulted that I was defeated by a boy. But now after I have heard about all his accomplishments from Prince Abdulla and now from you, I don't feel so insulted that I lost to boy. As a matter of fact, I feel thankful that he didn't kill me after I insulted him before the battle started'.

Khan Mohammed said to Zaki Khan, 'You are also a very formidable warrior, we have heard of your exploits over the years, tomorrow morning let us gather together and let us start working on a peace treaty that will benefit both Bastak and the Zand Dynasty, as this peace treaty will benefit all parties and should be beneficial for future generations in both Shiraz and Bastak, let us now have our dinner together and celebrate this great occasion that has brought us all together, to create an everlasting peace between our two peoples'.

That evening after dinner, Ali went back to his apartments in the palace to see Princess Fatima and his son Mohammed. He was very exhausted. As soon as Princess Fatima saw him, she said, 'you are so exhausted, why do you do this to yourself. Why don't you rest? You go from one city to the next, making these cities join Bastak creating this large empire for whom? And why? Ali said, 'I am doing this for everyone and especially for our children, I want the province to be safe, I want people to be able to travel from one city to the next without worrying that they would be attacked by any Bandits, I want to put a stop to all the wars between the different cities. We are all one people, but we spend our time fighting each other for more power. This is a problem that I would like to stop'.

Ali continued saying, 'So if the cost of peace and stability is a few sleepless nights and a little hard work, I say it is definitely worth it'. Princess Fatima said, 'I understand what you are doing is important, but I can't help worrying about you. Why did I fall in love with a man who thinks of others before he thinks of himself? I guess that is why I fell in love with you for that exact reason! Now I have to face the consequences of following my heart'. Ali said to Princess Fatima, 'I am sorry for being who I am but, one thing I will say, your life will be filled with excitement, there will never be a dull moment as long as I am with you my love'.

The next morning all parties met and started working diligently on the Peace treaty for days, then finally after 10 days of hard negotiations, discussions, and sleepless nights they all came to an agreement that seemed agreeable to all parties involved.

The Terms of the Treaty

1. The Bastaki Alliance will be called from now on (The Great State of Bastak) (دولة بستك العظمى).
2. The Great State of Bastak will have claim over all the cities, towns, villages, and Islands in the Hormozgan Province, without any objections from the Zand Dynasty.
3. All Prisoners of war that were taken during the Ashkenan Battle from the Zand army will be released.
4. All weapons taken from the Zand army after the surrender of the Zand army will be returned.
5. The Great State of Bastak will provide an army of 20,000 infantry and 5,000 cavalries, under the command of Ali BinAar or his successor, when needed by the Zand Dynasty to fight any aggressor against the Zand Dynasty.
6. Similarly, The Zand Dynasty will provide an army of 20,000 infantry and 5,000 cavalries to fight any aggressor against the Grate State of Bastak.
7. The Great State of Bastak will pay compensation of 25,000 Gold Coins to the Zand Dynasty for all the losses suffered by the army during the Ashkenan Battle.
8. The City of Ashkenan will be returned to Shiraz since it is not a part of the Hormozgan Province.
9. All people who wish to leave the city of Ashkenan before the handover can do so but they will forfeit the lands and properties to the state of Zand.
10. All weapons taken from the City of Ashkenan after the city had fallen will be returned to the state of Zand.

Once the treaty was approved by all parties it was sent to Vakil-Ol-Roaya Karim Khan Zand for his approval and signature. Zaki Khan sent a letter to Vakil-Ol-Roaya Karim Khan Zand, explaining the matter to him, and informing him of the benefits of this agreement, as they will gain a new and very powerful ally without losing anything of value to Zand, It has never been the plan of the Zand Dynasty to occupy the land requested by the Great State of Bastak, so giving the Hormozgan Province to at the Great State of Bastak, and having a very powerful army to help the Zand Dynasty at any time will be a great benefit to Shiraz and the Zand Dynasty.

Once Vakil-Ol-Roaya Karim Khan Zand was convinced that this treaty was beneficial to the Zand Dynasty, it was signed by Karim Khan and witnessed by his son and crown prince Abol-Fath Khan Zand in the year 1778.

Once the great state of Bastak was announced, all the terms and conditions of the peace treaty had to be fulfilled. So, the people of Ashkenan were informed that the city would be returned to the Zand dynasty, and if any person would like to relocate to any city that is under the great State of Bastak they can do so, and they will be given a piece of Land to build their house. But they will forfeit their lands and properties that they have in Ashkenan to the state of Zand.

Upon hearing this decree some 450 families mostly who were a part of the Ashkenan military, chose to leave the city of Ashkenan and join the Great State of Bastaks army, they chose to move to the city of Bastak. Khan Mohammed of Bastak promised to give them land and money to build their houses in Bastak and provide them with jobs in the Bastaki army. These families were so happy for the privilege of being a part of such a noble State as the people have always been treated with respect and freedom of speech and to do business without being over taxed by the government.

THE GREAT STATE OF BASTAK

When everyone arrived in Bastak after the declaration of the Great State of Bastak by the Zand Dynasty and the treaty signed by Vakil-Ol-Roaya Karim Khan Zand and witnessed by his son and crown prince Abol-Fath Khan Zand. Over the next year, many cities started to join the Great State of Bastak on their own, as with the treaty signed by the Zand Dynasty it made Bastak more legitimate and recognized by everyone that the Great State Bastak was now the new and official name of the Hormozgan Province.

By mid-1779, cities like Fatuyeh, Eelood, Merakan, Kanakh, Dezhgan, Gezir, Sayeh Khosh, Bostanu, Dogerdan, Qalat-e Bala, Qalat-e Pain, Keshar-e Olya, Hajiabad, Baqat, Gerdu, Bandzark, Gurzang, Kalut, Kong, Fakhrabad, Kariyan, Rudan, Jask, and four port cities had joined the Great State of Bastak, Bandar-e Lengeh, Bandar Moallem, Bandar e Khamir, also the islands of Ormus and Kish and finally the city with the largest port and largest population in the Hormozgan province Bandar Abbas, All these cities and port cities and Islands started joining the Great State of Bastak. They were all very happy to join as they felt that being a part of the Great State of Bastak would be beneficial for them and the Khans in all these cities didn't want to face the Bastaki army commanded by Ali BinAar after he defeated the Zand army commanded by the general Zaki Khan the terror of the Zand army who seized the former Safavid capital of Isfahan, and exploited mercilessly its population. No one of the Khans had the power to keep their current cities unless they aligned with the Great State of Bastak and requested to stay as Mayors of their cites Khan Mohammed agreed to keep them on as mayors of their respected cities, but the office of mayor was not to be inherited by their children, only people who were capable would be granted the status of Mayor of these cities, only if the children of the current Khans were capable of managing these cities as per the rules and regulations of the Great State of Bastak would be granted the status of Mayor of their cities after the retirement or death of their fathers.

It was a great time for the Great State of Bastak in less than one year more than 50 cities joined the Great State of Bastak to become a great force in the region. The

Great State of Bastak now had an army of more than 75,000 infantry and 10,000 cavalries. The Black Devils had now grown to 1,000 men. The fiercest Cavalry in the Hormozgan Province.

At this time Ali divided the army each city had a garrison of 1000 infantry and 200 cavalries. A large area in Bastak was made ready to house a permanent army. An infantry of 20,000 men, and cavalries of 5,000 men also stables to house 25,000 horses. Ali had an idea to create a mounted infantry to move the soldiers from one place to another in half the time it took to move a normal army, so all the infantry solders were given horses and trained in horse riding.

During this time, Ali and Princess Fatima were blessed with a new addition to the family, a baby girl and they named her Asma, now they were a family of four. When Asma was born, Haji Mohammed, Ali's mother Maryam and his brothers and sisters with all their families came to visit and see the new baby. It was a great time for Ali and Princess Fatima.

Haji Mohammed said to Ali, 'My son, I am very happy for you and your wife, but I would like to say that I am the proudest father in the world, to have you as my son. When people talk about you in BinAar and your achievements, there are no words that can describe my pride in being your father, I always thought of you as a hopeless person, a good for nothing spoiled Brat but you have proved to me and to the world that you are more capable than anyone, in this region'. Ali said, 'Father I am happy that you are proud of me. When I was young, I always felt like a big disappointment to you, as I didn't like doing the things you asked me to do'. Haji Mohammed said, 'now I understand that I was wrong pushing you to do things you were never meant to do, I thought that you should be like me and you should like the things I like. I never thought that you are a different person with your own likes and dislikes, you have your strengths that were not like my strengths and your brothers. But even in business you made more money in one trip to Anveh than any of your brothers has ever been able to do. You have achieved far greater respect and love than me and your older brothers by the people, because of you, the people in BinAar love and respect us, much more than before, and this is all because of your selfless actions in helping the people'.

Suddenly Ali's mother walked into the room, she looked at Haji Mohammed and said, 'stop lecturing my hero son. You still find faults in his actions'. Haji Mohammed smiled and said, 'Woman when have I have complained about Ali in the last three years, only to say I don't see him as much as before'. Ali's Mother said, 'Yes you haven't complained about Ali for a long time, I really miss those days when you both came to me complaining about each other, now all I get is your sisters and sister in-laws talking about what woman are saying about Ali and what Ali has done, I know my son is a hero, and all what woman want is for Ali to come to BinAar so that they could see him, you know Ali all the unmarried girls are in love with you and sometimes I feel that even the married ones are in love with you also, as they keep telling their husbands why don't you become more like Ali'.

Haji Mohammed said,' My son is a hero, what do you expect it is normal that people like him and want to copy him'. Ali's mother said, 'You remember a few years ago I tried to get you married to you cousin Fadilah, and she refused to marry you and said that she would rather stay unmarried then marry a spoiled brat like you, who does nothing just play with his guns and rides his hours all day long, she came to meet me the other day with her family, so I asked her does she still think My son Ali is a spoiled Brat? You know what she said, I was so stupid, you wanted me to marry Ali the great hero of BinAar and I refused and now look at me, I am marred to the biggest idiot in BinAar, who does nothing but sit all day with his other idiot friends and talk about Ali all day long, and what Ali plans to do next. I am so happy that people are sitting and strategizing about what Ali will do next, I was just laughing and laughing all day long, this news really made me happy that Allah proved everyone wrong who said that my Ali was a good for nothing'. Haji Mohammed said with a smile, 'now I know why you kept laughing and giggling when I came home that day, I didn't want to ask you the reason so not to upset you. I said to myself, 'If she is happy, that is good that means she is not angry with me'.

Ali's mother said, 'What do you mean not angry with me. Am I so scary that you are so afraid of me that you can't ask me why I am happy and why I am laughing?' Haji Mohammed said, 'Yes I don't like confrontations, so I prefer to be quite and not say anything'. As they were talking suddenly everyone walked into the majlis as they all wanted to talk to Ali and find out what are the plans of the government. With all this expansion going on will there be a new war for them to fight? Are there any cities that are not willing to join the Great State of Bastak? Ali looked at them and said don't worry we will not have a war with any city as with the current size of our army no city could stand before us with all their small armies'. Suddenly Hind Ali's sister said, 'which city has the guts to fight my brother Ali, who has never been defeated by any army in the past four years? My brother the HERO of Bastak'. So, Ali said 'my dear sister aren't you going to get married soon?' Hind looked at him and said, 'I will when I find another HERO like my brother Ali'. Ali's mother said, 'See how she answers this is what I keep getting from her for the past two years, she has refused so many men I don't think we have any more men in BinAar left that she hasn't refused to marry'. Ali Looked at Hind and said, 'I will find you a good husband that you can be proud of, someone who will love you and take great care of you my beloved and spoiled little sister'.

As they were talking a messenger came to Ali informing him that a delegation from Qalat-e Pain, had come to Bastak to join the great State of Bastak and Khan

Mohammed has requested your presence at the palace to receive the delegation. Ali asked his father Haji Mohammed 'would you like to come and see what happens when these cities come to join Bastak?' Haji Mohammed said, 'I would be happy to come, I hope this will not create any problems for you my son', Ali said, 'you are most welcome to come my father, let us go so you can see what happens and tell mother and the rest about it'.

As they entered the grand Majlis everyone was waiting for Ali to arrive before letting the delegation enter. Khan Mohammed, Crown Prince Abdulla, all the commanders and the ministers were all present, only the commander of the army Ali was not present. So as soon as Ali entered Khan Mohammed gave the order to let the delegation from Qalat-e Pain to enter. As soon as they entered Khalil Khan was looking for just one person, he greeted Khan Mohammed and said, 'could you please introduce me to your great commander Ali BinAar, I would like to meet him, as I have been hearing everything about him for the past 4 years. Khan Mohammed said, Khalil Khan please meet Ali BinAar, Haji Mohammed was looking at what was happening and Khalil Khan instead of shaking Ali's hand he just embraced Ali and said, 'This is the first time I have seen you but I have been waiting for this day for so many years ever since I started hearing about your exploits, every time you won a battle, I felt like it was my son winning the battle and felt so proud, you can't imagine how much'. Khalil Khan met all the other commanders, and said it gives me great pleasure to announce that Qalat-e Pain would like to join the great state of Bastak.

That night when Ali and Haji Mohammed were going back to Ali's house, Haji Mohammed said, 'I couldn't believe what I saw today in the grand majlis,' Ali said, 'what do you mean Father?' Haji Mohammed said, 'Khalil Khan came to Bastak to join the Great State of Bastak, and meet you, A man who is supposed to be your enemy, as soon as he meets you, he embraces you like you were his son that he hadn't seen for a long time, does this thing happen a lot or was this the first time?' Ali said, 'This is what normally happens they all feel the need to embrace me, I don't know why! But the older Khans feel I am like their son and the younger Khans feel I am like their younger brother but most of them have to embrace me, is it out of love or respect I don't know but they all seem to really love me, I am still thinking about it, maybe you could ask them about it, I feel embarrassed to say anything'.

When they reached home Haji Mohammed informed everyone about what he saw, Ali's mother said, 'I am happy that all the people who were your enemies in the past now love you like you are a part of their family this is good'. Princess Fatima said, 'I don't know why but I feel very uncomfortable when these things happen, I feel that it is a show that these Khans are creating just to make people believe that they are genuine, but the fact of the matter is that they are actually losing their grip over their cities, and everything is now under the Great State of Bastak. Hind said, 'I think they just want to meet this great man who is responsible for taking away their power and their grip over their cities without even going to war with them. Because of Ali they are now powerless to even say I don't want to join the Great State of Bastak, they know that even the Zand army that was almost double the size of the Bastaki army lost to Ali, so what chance do they have fighting Ali, and that is why they feel the need to embrace Ali for the fear he has put in their hearts and minds'. Ali said to Hind, 'My baby sister, I must say that is very deep and I think that you have understood the situation better than me'.

The next morning celebrations had started in Bastak as another city was joining the great state of Bastak. This meant that a delegation from Bastak had to go to Qalat-e Pain, to meet the people headed by Prince Abdulla and Ali with his Black Devils. A great spectacle had to be created for the people for them to feel that they are a part of something great so 20,000 infantry and 5,000 cavalries will also join this great delegation. This is now the normal practice for all new cities joining the Great State of Bastak. The people had to feel safe and happy with all the new changes that were happening, they had to see a part of the strength of Bastak.

Prince Abdulla always wore white, and he had a white horse, Ali always wore Black and had a Black horse, also all the Black Devils wore Black and had black horses. The only difference was that Ali's horse would dance and walk sideways. That is how people knew who Ali was when they saw him on his dancing horse. As soon as Ali would pass by the people, they would start singing a song the people had created.

'He fights for the people, he never asks for any reward,

Ali BinAar is our Hero, he protects us with his sword,

He defeated Zaki Khan and all the other Khans surrendered to him'

He created the Great State of Bastak, after the Zand army was defeated by him'.On this Trip Ali asked his entire family to join him before they went back to BinAar. Ali wanted his family to see this new city and join in the celebrations as they may not get another chance to have such fun, being treated like VIPs in a city they may never visit again. Princess Fatima said to Ali's mother, 'Look at how the people love him, only one thing I don't like is that all the young girls just scream when he passes by. I know he doesn't look at them, but he is only human and some of them are really beautiful'. Ali's mother said, 'don't worry, Ali only loves you and he will never look at another woman, I know my son he has never been one to chase women'. Princess Fatima said, 'I hope you are right; I sometimes get these bad dreams that he is married to a second wife'. Ali's mother said, 'Ali and a second wife this can never happen he loves you a lot to have that happen'.

Ali and his family spent a week in Qalat-e Pain, they really had fun and then they left, and everyone went to BinAar, only Ali and his family went back to Bastak. After they arrived the next day, they received a letter from Zaki Khan informing them that Vakil-Ol-Roaya Karim Khan Zand, had died a few days ago he was suffering from Tuberculosis.

ZAKI KHAN AND THE SETTLEMENT OF IZADKHWAST

Zaki Khan was a major participant in the political power struggles that followed the death of Karim Khan on 2nd March 1779. The most famous thing that Zaki Khan did was when he baited Shaykh Ali Khan and Nazar Ali Khan out of the fortress of Shiraz, and slaughtered them, so he could put Karim Khan's two sons Abol-Fath Khan Zand, and youngest son Mohammad Ali Khan Zand as the new Zand dynasty's joint rulers.

During this time, the Qajar Prince Agha Muhammad Khan, Whom Karim Khan had retained as a hostage in Shiraz to prevent any rebellions from his clan the Qajar's, managed to escape from Shiraz and went to his stronghold. To catch Agha Muhammad Khan, Zaki Khan sent his nephew, Ali Murad Khan to catch him and bring him back. But as soon as Ali Murad Khan reached Isfahan he mutinied against his uncle, at the same time Sadiq Khan was gathering an army in the southeast to remove Zaki Khan as regent. Zaki Khan decided to deal with Ali Murad Khan first in Isfahan then go after Sadiq Khan.

Zaki Khan sent a letter to Khan Mohammed requesting him to send an army as per the treaty agreement. as the army was housed in Bastak of 20,000 mounted infantry and 5,000 cavalries. With 15 cannons. A 10-day march would now take four to five days, this made moving the army from one place to another much faster. When the Bastaki army arrived in Shiraz, Zaki Khan was amazed at the speed the army arrived, after he met and greeted Ali BinAar, Zaki Khan asked Ali, 'how did you manage this miracle by reaching so fast to Shiraz, I was expecting you to arrive next week?' Ali said, 'I put the infantry on horses so now they can travel at the same speed of the cavalries, so I don't have to split the army in half and send the cavalry in advance of the infantry, also when the infantry arrives, they are fresh and can fight without resting'.

Zaki Khan said, 'It's good you have arrived 1 week early, now we can move much faster than expected. Let us leave Shiraz in two days. In the meantime, let me show you the most beautiful city in the world, Shiraz. Zaki Khan took Ali on a tour of Shiraz so that he would see the wonders of Shiraz and see what his brother Karim Khan Zand had built after its destruction. Ali said to Zaki Khan, 'Shiraz is truly a beautiful city and I wish more cities were as beautiful'.

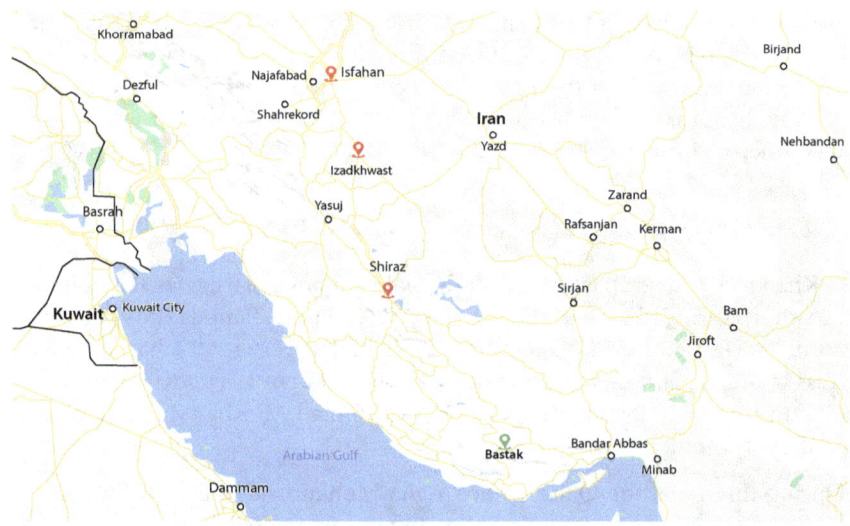

Ali noticed some changes in Zaki Khan, he was not the same man whom he had met in Ashkenan 10 months ago. He looked more frustrated and short-tempered; any small thing would upset him. Zaki Khan and Ali BinAar left Shiraz with an army of 60,000 infantry, 10,000 cavalry and 40 cannons. Ali's army, being more mobile, went ahead and they had agreed to meet at a settlement called Izadkhwast, it is 135 km south of Isfahan.

When Ali reached the settlement of Izadkhwast, he set up camp awaiting the arrival of the Zand army. During this time Ali met with the people of Izadkhwast, he visited their homes and helped some people who needed help. After three days when Zaki Khan arrived, he started attacking and killing the people of Izadkhwast some of whom Ali had just helped, this made Ali very angry he asked Zaki Khan, 'why are you killing these innocent people'. Zaki Khan said, 'because I can. I have to show these people who is in command'. Ali said, 'I can never support brutality just to put fear in people's hearts, this is not the right thing to do'. Zaki Khan's own men were shocked at this behavior, that a group of tribal leaders were so angry at Zaki Khan that during the night they murdered Zaki Khan as he was resting in his tent.

In the morning Ali and his men got the news that Zaki Khan had been murdered during the night by one of the tribal leaders, Ali decided to leave as the war for the Bastaki army was over with the death of Zaki Khan. Since Ali had a very mobile army, he reached Bastak in half the normal time. When Khan Mohammed met Ali after he got back from Izadkhwast he asked him what happened, 'Ali said that the way Zaki Khan was acting I feel that he had lost his head, and when he started killing those poor people in Izadkhwast It was really unbearable. In a way I am happy that Zaki Khan was killed'. Princess Fatima was happy that Ali was back home safely.

A few months later in the same year 1779, Sadeq Khan Zand, after defeating Ali Murad Khan Zand, in an epic battle became the new ruler of the Zand Dynasty. Again, after two years in 1781, Sadeq khan died, and he was succeeded as the ruler of the Zand Dynasty by Ali Murad Khan Zand in 1782.

It was a great time for Bastak, as time went by the Great State of Bastak started to grow more and more as new cities started to join, Bastak became the most powerful force with the largest army and Ali BinAar was the greatest undefeated commander of that time in the region.

Ali's adventures continued over the next 25 years, Princess Fatima gave Ali five children. (The oldest was a boy named Mohammed, then three girls Asma, Amira, and Adila and finally she gave birth to a boy and named him Abdi). It was a happy time for Ali BinAar, his family, and the Great State of Bastak.

The next Great Adventure will be
(The Adventures of Ali BinAar 2 and the City of Minab).

THE FAMILY TREE

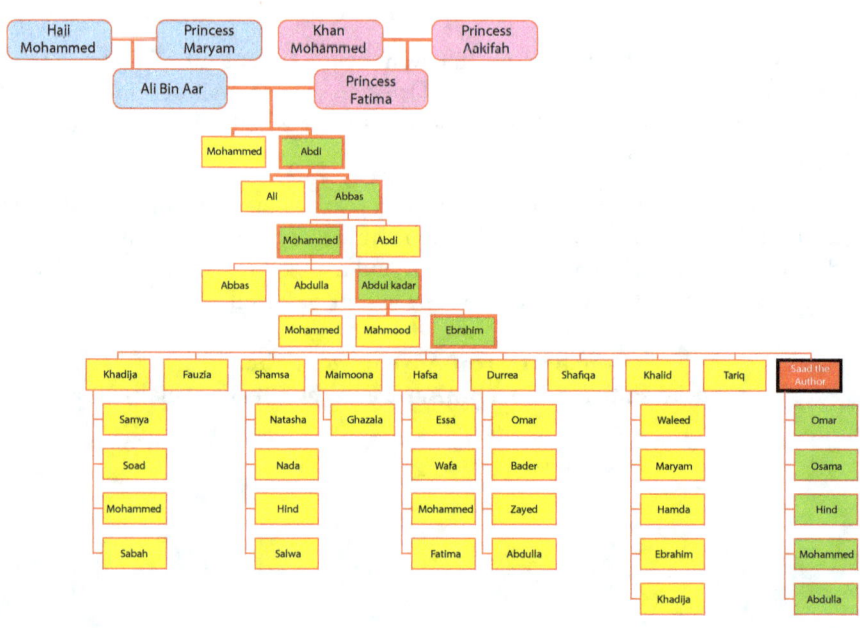